THE BAKER'S BODYGUARD

SUTTON CAPITAL SERIES BOOK 3

LORI RYAN

ALSO BY LORI RYAN

The Sutton Capital Series

Legal Ease

Penalty Clause

The Baker's Bodyguard (A Sutton Capital Series Novella)

Negotiation Tactics

The Billionaire's Suite Dreams

The Baker, the Bodyguard, and the Wedding Bell Blues (A Sutton Capital Series Novella)

Her SEALed Fate

The Sutton Capital Series Boxed Set (Books One Through Four)

The Sutton Capital Series Boxed Set (Books Five Through Seven)

Sutton Capital Intrigue

Cutthroat

Cut and Run

Cut to the Chase

Sutton Capital On the Line Series

Pure Vengeance

Latent Danger

Wicked Justice

Heroes of Evers, Texas Series

Love and Protect

Promise and Protect

Honor and Protect (An Evers, TX Novella)

Serve and Protect

Desire and Protect

Cherish and Protect

Triple Play Curse Series

Game Changer

Game Maker

Game Clincher

The Triple Play Curse Boxed Set

Standalone Books

Stealing Home (writing in Melanie Shawn's Hope Falls Series)

Any Witch Way (writing in Robyn Peterman's Magic and Mayhem Series)

All In (writing in the Sleeper SEALs Series)

The Baker's Bodyguard
by Lori Ryan

ISBN: 978-0-9892453-5-7

ACKNOWLEDGMENTS

I'd like to thank my husband and children for their never-ending patience. You truly amaze me. Thank you to my beta readers on this project, Susan Smith and Patty Parent. You guys are invaluable on every project I work on. And thank you to Bev Harrison for her input and editing services.

CHAPTER 1

*J*essica Bradley stared at herself in the mirror, hating what she saw looking back at her. In the past nine months since her sister, Kelly, had been kidnapped, Jesse had become a frightened, anxiety-ridden mess. It didn't matter that she hadn't been the one to be kidnapped. It didn't matter that Kelly had been rescued and was now safe. It didn't matter that Jesse had played a role in bringing Kelly home.

So slowly she'd scarcely noticed it, Jesse had stopped leaving the house unless she was with someone else. She wasn't agoraphobic. She left the house – just not alone. At first, she hadn't realized she was acting differently. She had nightmares, reliving the terrifying day when they knew Kelly had been taken but didn't know why; reliving the agonizing moment when they realized Kelly had been taken by people who intended to sell her in a human trafficking ring. That there would be no ransom.

Then Jesse began to have flashes of anxiety when a stranger approached to ask her the time, or someone bumped into her in the line at the coffee store. She gradually began to commute to work with her dad, citing savings in gas and convincing him to drive five minutes past his office to drop her off at the bakery where she worked. She only went out with friends if they could pick her up and take her home afterward, so she wouldn't have to be alone at any time.

And tonight, when she'd momentarily lost her friends in a large dance club, she'd had such a panic attack she thought she was going to crawl under the table and hide. If her friend, Sarah, hadn't come back when she did, Jesse is fairly sure she would have either thrown up or begun to cry.

The whole thing made Jesse feel so...so...just, stupid, really. And humiliated. How could she tell anyone what was going on without people thinking she was a first-class idiot?

It wasn't you they took!

Jesse wanted to scream at herself. I have no right to be so scared, so affected by this, she thought as she looked in the mirror.

This cowardly, quiet person wasn't her at all. Jesse had always been friendly and outgoing. She'd invariably been the kind of person you could count on when you needed help with something. When a friend was going through a hard time, she'd be the one holding their hand, cheering them on. She was bubbly and fun, and she'd finally had a direction in her life. She was active and friendly and went after what she wanted in life. Until now.

Jesse had gotten her undergrad degree in business administration from the University of Connecticut, but then hadn't really been happy with the work she was doing after graduation. She didn't do well stuck in an office day after day. A year before Kelly's kidnapping, she'd gone home to live with her parents so she could follow her passion. She wanted to bake. Not just bake – she wanted to create. To make people swoon when they took a bite of one of her desserts.

She'd gotten an entry-level job in a bakery, helping in the mornings with the baking and then working the counter in the afternoon. She'd applied to a pastry chef program in New York City, and had been all set to start before the kidnapping. The combination of that program with her undergrad meant she could start her own bakery.

But then Kelly was taken, and Jesse deferred her acceptance – twice.

Jesse heard a light tapping on the door and her mother's voice.

"Are you still up, honey?" her mother asked through the door.

Jesse wanted to remain silent and pretend to be asleep, but the light was on.

"Yeah, Mom. I'm up," she said as she opened the door.

Her mother looked at her with those eyes that saw too much, knew too much. "Are you all right, Jess? You seemed upset when you came in tonight."

"I'm fine, Mom." Jesse pasted a smile on her face, but even she knew it was a weak one. "I'm just tired. I probably shouldn't have gone out tonight at all."

Her mother looked at her a beat too long before saying goodnight. Jesse knew her mother had begun to notice the patterns. The way Jesse made an excuse to stay home if she weren't able to drive with someone. The way she never took the bus anywhere anymore or went out for runs like she used to. The only problem was, Jesse didn't know what to do to fix the problem, and she didn't know how to tell her mom and dad what was going on.

Jesse closed the door and pulled back the covers on her bed. She opened her closet door and looked to be sure no one was inside. Tears began to stream down her face as she went through the ritual that let her sleep at night. She opened the bathroom door and pulled the shower curtain aside. Empty.

Jesse left the bathroom light on and the door ajar. She pulled the bed skirt up from the floor and bent to look under the bed. Nothing there. She curled up in bed and shut off the lamp. And she cried.

CHAPTER 2

*J*ack Sutton sat at his desk looking over reports from one of the fledgling businesses his company had funded. They were on track and meeting expectations so far, but Jack would keep a close eye on things to be sure everything stayed that way. Investing in new enterprises – as opposed to providing money for growth or expansion – was always risky. New businesses had a high rate of failure, and if the business failed, so did Jack and the investors who counted on him.

The intercom on Jack's desk buzzed, and his receptionist's voice came through the line.

"Jack, your mother-in-law is here to see you. Can I send her in?"

Jack frowned. Betty never visited him at the office.

"Yes. Is she all right? Is something wrong?"

"She says she's fine. She just needs a minute."

Jack didn't answer. He was already at the door to his office, pulling it open to get to Betty Bradley, his wife's mother and a woman he'd grown incredibly close to in the past year.

"Mom, is everything okay?" Jack asked as he crossed the lobby to meet Betty halfway.

"It's fine, Jack. I'm sorry to drop in unannounced like this and worry you. I just wanted to talk to you without bothering Kelly. Do you have a minute?"

Jack smiled as he led Betty into his office. "Always, Mom, you know that."

Jack had lost his own mom before Kelly and he met, and Kelly's mom had become as much a mother to him as his own had been. He'd been amazed at how readily she'd taken him in as one of her own, and how easily he'd felt a part of Kelly's family.

They sat on the couch along one wall of Jack's office.

"Can I get you anything? Do you want some coffee or water?"

Kelly's mom shook her head, and Jack could see there was more to this visit than she was letting on. She was worried about something.

"What is it, Mom? What's wrong?" Jack asked gently.

"It's Jesse. I don't want Kelly to worry, but I don't know what to do, Jack. I don't know how to help her."

Jack leaned toward Betty, his arms resting on his knees as he listened.

"What's happening with Jesse? We just saw her the other day, and she seemed fine."

"That's just it. She's okay when she's with one of us or when she's at home. The changes are so subtle it took me a long time to notice it. Too long. I should have seen what was happening right after Kelly was taken, but the truth is, I was so caught up in making sure Kelly was okay, I think Jesse slipped through the cracks," Betty said, her face a mask of guilt.

"Tell me what changes you mean." Jack was confused. He'd seen Jesse almost weekly now that Kelly was pregnant.

She might be a bit more subdued at times than she was when he'd first met her—

No, wait. Now that he thought about it, she was a lot more subdued than she normally was. Jack frowned. How had he missed that?

"I think she was more affected by Kelly's...by the incident than we realized." Jack knew Kelly's mom didn't like to talk about the kidnapping. She often just called it "that time" or "the incident" rather than saying the 'k' word. Jack could understand. It was hard for all of them to deal with the fear they felt that day. Jack just wasn't a person to hide from things, so he called it what it was and didn't pussyfoot around it.

"I think we all were. I mean, hell, I didn't sleep the same for a long time after we got her back. I'd imagine Jesse had a hard time, too, but I guess I never thought to ask her. You think she's still struggling with it?" Jack asked.

"Jack, I don't think she's dealt with it at all. It took me a while to figure out what was going on. Jesse doesn't leave the house without one of us or a friend with her. Last week, one of her friends was supposed to pick her up for a lunch date with a group she hadn't seen in a long time. I know she was looking forward to seeing the girls. They were people she went to school with. Her friend called at the last minute and said she couldn't get her and asked if she could drive over herself. Jesse backed out. She said she decided she was too tired from work the day before, but that's not true, Jack. I saw the panic. She didn't want to go by herself.

She came home from a club with some friends the other night, and I could tell she was upset. She told me she was just tired. I called her friend the next day and asked if something had happened. She told me she came back to their table to find Jesse alone and in a complete panic. She said Jesse looked terrified. But, Jesse told her she wasn't feeling well, and her friend brought her home early. She's trying to hide it, but I think something's wrong, Jack."

Jack felt horrible. "I never even thought to make sure Jesse was okay. Kelly saw a counselor, and she's in a support group. She had a bodyguard with her for a long time until she felt safe going out alone. Honestly, I still have someone tail her from a distance, but that's for my sake, not hers. I was a wreck every time she left the house alone after Zach stopped going with her. Looking back, it makes sense that Jesse would have had trouble dealing with it. I'm so sorry we didn't think about that, Betty."

Jack was a man to jump in and fix things. He believed there was always a solution, and he didn't sit back to wait for someone else to solve problems.

"Is Jesse still working at the bakery?" Jack asked.

"Yes. In fact, that's another thing. That job was supposed to be temporary. She wanted to get some experience before she went to pastry school, but she seems to have abandoned that dream. She seems content now to follow someone else's recipes in someone else's bakery. That's not Jesse at all. She was meant to be making her own recipes, finding her own way, not following someone else. She hasn't talked about pastry school in ages."

"What school was she supposed to go to?" The beginnings of an idea were starting to come together in Jack's head. He just needed to figure out all the pieces.

"The International Culinary Academy in New York. She's deferred twice. She should be starting in two weeks but she never confirmed her registration, and I think her acceptance has probably lapsed now."

Jack kissed Betty on the cheek. "Don't worry. I've got a plan. I'll talk to Jesse when we come to dinner Sunday. The bodyguard we used for Kelly, Zach Harris, also focuses on recovery by working with crisis counselors and teaching self-defense. Then he gradually eases people back into their day-to-day lives. I'll call him and get his help on this. I'll see you guys Sunday, okay?"

Betty smiled at Jack and hugged him. "My Kelly got so lucky the day she met you, Jack."

Jack just laughed. He knew he was the lucky one.

CHAPTER 3

*J*esse loved Sunday dinners at her parents' house. Her brothers, Liam and David, came over whenever they weren't traveling for work. It was always funny to see her mom grill them about whom they were dating and when they'd settle down.

Jack and Kelly came almost every week now, too. Jesse loved seeing them and couldn't wait for their baby to be born. Sundays were the time she felt the safest now. Surrounded by her family in her parents' home. On Sundays, she felt as if she could breathe again.

Jesse was rolling up the last of her knotted garlic rolls for dinner when she heard the front door open and her mother's voice mingling with those of Kelly and Jack. Minutes later, the kitchen was full as the family gathered. Jesse popped the sheet of rolls in the oven as she let the chatter and laughter surround her like a comfy blanket.

She was surprised when her brother-in-law suddenly singled her out.

"Hey, Jess. You got a minute? I have an idea I want to talk to you about," Jack said, drawing looks from everyone around him. Except her mother, Jesse noticed. Her mother was carefully looking anywhere in the room other than at Jack and Jesse.

Jesse swallowed her annoyance with her mother and followed Jack out to the back porch.

"What's up?" Jesse sat on one gliding rocker while Jack took the other.

"I have a proposition for you, Jess. There's a little convenience store in the bottom of the Sutton Capital office building. They sell papers, coffee, bagels, things like that. The same guy has been running it for years, but he and his wife are ready to retire. I need to find someone new to run it, but I have a better idea if you'll help me."

Jesse narrowed her eyes at Jack. "Why do you need to find someone?"

"I own the building," Jack said so simply he made Jesse laugh.

"Of course you do. I forgot who I was dealing with."

Jack smiled. "It was a good investment. Sutton uses the top three floors, and we lease out the rest of the space to other companies."

"Okay," Jess smiled at her brother-in-law. "But what does that have to do with me?"

"I want to turn the convenience store into a bakery. There's a little room to expand it, and we can knock out the outer wall that faces the street and put in a glass front and door to open it up to street traffic as well. I was thinking baked goods and coffee in the morning—"

Before he could finish, Jesse took over. "Paninis and sandwiches for lunch."

"Exactly," said Jack with a smile.

"Oh. Okay. Well, I can help you find someone, I guess. I'll see if my boss knows any pastry chefs in the area looking for work," Jesse said.

She would kill for the job herself, but she still hadn't gone to school to cap off the experience she'd gotten at her job at the bakery. Not to mention, taking this on would mean driving herself there alone every day, and working alone while she got the bakery set up and running. Even after it got to the point of needing employees, it would likely mean several hours a day when she was there without anyone else. She'd have to work before and after hours getting the pastries and breads baked, decorating cakes and cookies, running the books.

Jesse blinked back tears as she tried to swallow the pain. Why couldn't she just get over this damn fear and get back out in the world? If she could only get past her anxiety, she would have been able to ask Jack to at least let her work there as an assistant baker and help get things started. If it weren't for this fear, she would have finished her training at the Culinary Academy several months ago. She could have run the whole project for Jack.

Jack pulled Jesse from her thoughts. "No, Jess," Jack laughed. "I want you to run it. I'll put up the money for the renovations and get things ready for you while you're in New York at the Academy. I checked with them, and they still have space for you to start in two weeks. The build-out will take a while so it won't be a problem to wait for you to get back."

Oh no. How do I tell Jack I'm too afraid to go to school or live alone, much less go to New York?

Before Jesse could figure out how to say no without telling Jack the humiliating truth, Jack reached over and took her hand and squeezed.

"I won't send you alone, Jess. Remember Zach? Kelly's bodyguard after the kidnapping? I spoke with him, and he's all set to go with you. You'll have a suite of rooms at one of Gabe Sawyer's hotels so Zach can stay with you, but you'll still have privacy." Jack's friend Gabe Sawyer owned a string of hotels across the country.

Jesse swallowed. Jack was speaking so gently – he had to know.

"Jess, it's okay. The kidnapping was hard on all of us. We should have seen that something wasn't right a lot sooner than this. I'm so sorry we didn't help you earlier."

Jesse felt tears start to stream down her cheeks. She couldn't speak past the lump in her throat, but she didn't need to. Jack kept speaking quietly.

"Zach did a lot more for Kelly than just guard her. He helped her learn self-defense, helped ease her into doing things on her own. He got her into a counseling group and helped her find a therapist she liked working with. He'll be able to do the same thing for you. He'll also go with you to class every day until you're able to go alone. You won't have to do things on your own until you're ready."

"I feel so stupid, Jack. I wasn't even the one that was taken, and it was almost a year ago. I don't know why I can't get over it," Jesse practically whispered the confession. She couldn't make eye contact with Jack. It was too mortifying to have him and the rest of her family know what was going on.

"Hey, Jess. There's nothing to be embarrassed about. Hell, I had nightmares for months after Kelly came home. I still have one of Zach's people following her, and that's mostly for my comfort. We should have helped you a lot earlier, but I won't let you go through this alone now. Promise."

"What if I get to New York and I can't get through the program? What if I freeze-up there?" Jesse had stopped crying and looking at Jack was getting easier, but she still felt nervous. She couldn't believe Jack would do all this for her.

"If you need more time, just take it. I'll get someone to run your bakery for you until you can do it. And, Zach will be with you every step of the way," Jack said.

"My bakery?" Jess laughed. "It's your bakery."

"Nope. The whole thing's going in your name. Get through school and you've got your own business to come back to,"

Jesse's jaw hit the floor. "What do you mean? Jack, that's crazy! You can't do that."

Jack shrugged, as if it were perfectly normal to give away hundreds of thousands of dollars. "Sure I can. You're my sister. If that isn't reason enough, consider it a belated thank you for getting Kelly back to me. We would never have found her if you hadn't figured out that Kelly was signaling us. Chad and I were ready to dismiss Kelly's clue completely. I owe you everything, Jess. I owe you Kelly's life and my life. A bakery is nothing compared to what you've given me."

Jess sat stunned until Jack stood and put out his hand for hers to lead her back into the house, where he announced his plan for the bakery to everyone. He skipped the part where she was going to need an armed escort just to get through classes, but Jess saw a small look pass between her mother and Jack. Suddenly, it wasn't so hard to know that her mother and Jack knew her secret. Instantly, Jesse felt hopeful.

CHAPTER 4

*Z*ach pulled his car up to the front of the large white house in Hamden, Connecticut and shut off the engine. He'd never turn down a job from Jack Sutton, but he had a feeling this was going to be one of the hardest jobs he'd ever worked. Jesse Bradley would challenge his rule never to mix business with pleasure like no woman ever had.

He'd met Jesse several times when he'd been working with Jack's wife, Kelly. Every time he saw her, she took his breath away. Just being in the same room with her had him on edge and distracted. Not really the best state of mind for keeping someone safe. The hardest part about this job would be the challenge of coaching her and helping her get past her fears. He'd get her into professional counseling, of course, but they'd also work closely together to practice self-defense. He'd teach her how to be aware of her surroundings without being a paranoid ball of nerves. He'd help her to gradually take on a bit more independence until she was ready to stand on her own.

He'd done that with dozens of clients. Victims of violent attacks or kidnappings. Each time, a closeness was developed. It was never sexual. It was just a bond that developed when you help someone past their fears and work so closely together.

But Jesse was walking, talking sex appeal. She had hair that bordered somewhere between brown and blonde. Almost like honey. She had these big blue eyes that he wanted to get lost in. And she was tiny. So tiny he wanted to wrap her up and protect her from the world. And when she smiled at him...

Hell, who was he kidding? He was a dead man. He didn't have any defenses when Jesse smiled at him.

Zach cut the ignition and walked up to the front door. Steeling himself, he rang the bell and stood back to wait. Then, there it was. That smile. Those eyes. He felt as if he'd been knocked out and splayed out on the front steps for everyone to see.

"Zach," Jesse said softly and smiled that killer smile at him. The one that made him feel as if he were the only man on earth.

He hoped she didn't notice he was practically holding his breath for fear of breathing in the smell that always seemed to surround her. Sugar and cinnamon. As if she'd been baking all day. She used to bring muffins and pastries to the house for Kelly, and she always shared with him. He'd had to increase his workout just to make up for all her treats he could never resist.

Zach cleared his throat and tried for casual. "Hey, Jesse. How've you been?"

I FORGOT. In all my worry about this trip and going to school and being out in the world again, I plain freaking forgot the effect Zach Harris has on me.

Jesse stepped back into the house. Partly to let Zach in, and partly out of self-preservation. When Zach was in the room, she became a bubbly, babbling idiot.

Here, taste this pastry, Zach. Oh, did you see the pie I baked, Zach? Look at these cookies, Zach. Have some.

It was as if she couldn't control what came out of her mouth around him. And she seemed to have this uncontrollable urge to feed him sweets. She knew what that was. It was her own personal form of sexual frustration. The more the attraction and frustration, the sweeter the goodies. The last time she'd seen Zach Harris several months ago, she'd made him tarts with a flourless chocolate filling and homemade raspberry sauce. Sure, she'd brought them over under the guise of letting Kelly try a new recipe, but she knew the truth. They were sex tarts for Zach.

Zach wasn't what you would typically expect in a bodyguard. He was just shy of six feet tall with dark blond hair that was a little long and shaggy. Unruly, some might call it. To Jesse, it was nothing but hot. It made her want to run her fingers through the wayward curls and try to tame them. He had deep-brown eyes and tanned skin. He was strong and lean and muscled from top to bottom, but he wasn't huge. His strength was...unassuming. You'd look at him, and you'd never guess he could level a man twice his size without breaking a sweat.

Jesse saw it happen one day. When Kelly was rescued, they kept most of the newspapers and tabloids away from her, but one paparazzo got by. He jumped out in front of Kelly and Jesse when they were walking into the house, and Zach flattened the guy with what seemed like a flick of his wrist. It was literally the coolest thing Jess had ever seen. That day, she'd felt safe.

Jesse pulled herself out of her thoughts when she realized Zach had asked her something. "Um...what?"

Zach smiled that gorgeous, easy, bone-melting smile. "I asked how you've been. Although, I guess I know the answer to that. Jack told me you've been having some trouble. I wish I'd have known about it sooner; I would've come."

Jesse blinked at Zach.

Come? For me?

Suddenly, Jesse's cheeks were burning as the double meaning of those words sank in.

Oh, God. Get it together, Jess. That's not what he meant. Oh, no! Now I'm picturing him naked!

Jess backed up until the back of her knees hit the couch, and she sank down into it. She was struggling to come up with some answer. Something to say to the quizzical look Zach was now giving her, when Kelly and Jack came into the room.

"Zach!" Kelly threw her arms around Zach and hugged him tight, and Jesse knew the answering grin on his face was genuine.

Jack shook hands with Zach, and Jesse and Kelly's mom came from the kitchen to welcome the man who would now be guarding a second of her daughters. Zach was beginning to look a bit overwhelmed by all the hugs and attention. Jesse was used to seeing that look on peoples' faces when they were in her parents' home. Her whole family was loud and demonstrative and loved to welcome people as one of their clan. And the man who was going to help her daughter was getting a double dose of love from Mamma Bradley at the moment.

Jess was just trying to recover and get her wits about her. They had a two-hour drive ahead of them. Enough time for Jesse to put her foot in her mouth and humiliate the crap out of herself with steamy, inappropriate fantasies about the guy who was assigned to take care of her. Her babysitter.

Great. I'm lusting after my babysitter.

Through the whole lunch her mother had laid out on the back patio before she and Zach took off for New York, Jess kept her mind busy thinking of ideas for new recipes.

Devil's food cupcakes with a cream cheese frosting center. Cream cheese frosting with chocolate shavings.

Buttermilk pie with a pecan walnut crust.

Triple chocolate cheesecake with caramel ribbon on top. No, wait. Dulce de Leches cheesecake with caramel ribbon on top. Oh hell, I'll make them both.

CHAPTER 5

Zach pulled up to the front of the hotel and turned the keys over to the valet. Their bags were whisked away to be brought to their suite, so Jesse entered the lobby with nothing more than Zach by her side and her purse in her hands. She clutched the purse in front of her as if it could shield her from the new surroundings.

Zach placed his hand on her shoulder and steered her to the front desk where the manager met them to welcome them to the hotel. Apparently, when you're friends with the hotel's owner, and you've been given the penthouse to use for six months, you get a very warm welcome from the management.

Jesse felt better the minute they were handed key fobs for the elevator and stairwell access points. The elevator wouldn't allow access to their floor without the key fob and the stairwells on their floor only opened from the inside unless you had a key fob. Either she or Zach would need to let any visitors in.

"Mr. Sutton asked that we stock the penthouse kitchen for you in case Ms. Bradley wants to cook or bake. It's got everything we thought you might need, but you can always call down if you find you're missing something. And, of course, room service is available to you at any time as well," explained the manager.

"Thank you," murmured Jesse. She wasn't used to people waiting on her like this. Between having Zach drive her around and the hotel staff kowtowing to her every need, Jesse felt more and more like a fish out of water with every passing minute.

But then Zach's hand was on her shoulder again, warm and strong, and she began to feel more grounded. It struck Jesse as a very nonsexual touch. She guessed it was meant to be platonic. Simply to guide but not be intimate the way a hand on her back might be. It didn't work. Zach was sex incarnate, so even the most utilitarian of touches seemed highly-charged coming from him.

They walked to the elevator together and got on. Sure enough, the elevator wouldn't register that they had pushed the penthouse button until Zach swiped his fob over the sensor pad.

"We should probably drop your car off when we visit home some weekend. Maybe in a couple of weeks? We won't have so much luggage then so we can just take the train back," Jesse said. She wondered if Zach knew she was trying to fill the space with something other than drooling all over him in her head. It was getting hard to function with all the fantasies she had going on up there. Most of them involved his hands on every part of her body. Followed by his mouth. His tongue. A grazing of teeth.

So, yup, talking about the car seemed like the best strategy.

"It might be nice for us to have it. In case you end up being too uncomfortable on the subway in the beginning. We don't know how you're going to react to any of this stuff," Zach said.

Jesse frowned. "I hadn't thought about the subway."

The idea that she might be too freaked out by taking mass transit to school or appointments with her counselor, even with Zach with her, was depressing. That's when Jesse made a decision.

"Uh uh. No way in hell I'm letting this cripple me that much. I'll put my big girl panties on. We're riding the damn subway." Jesse saw Zach's grin as she moved off the elevator, but then she stopped short. The elevator opened straight into the penthouse suite. It was utterly stunning.

"Holy monkey butts. This place is amazing." Jesse stood with Zach beside her taking it all in. He looked completely unimpressed, but he was probably used to escorting dignitaries and famous people into hotel rooms like this.

For Jesse, the experience was totally new. The top-floor suite was opulence personified. Floor-to-ceiling windows looked out onto the brightly-lit cityscape below them, sparkling and shining. The lighting in the suite was subdued, with tan overtones that highlighted the soft, inviting furniture. The kitchen was small but modern, calling to Jesse. Everywhere she looked, granite or marble surfaces gleamed; wood was polished to an impeccable shine, and pillows were fluffed to the max.

Zach walked around Jesse and crossed to the room on the right, opening the door. He quickly scanned the room, checked the bathroom and closet.

"This one's yours, Jesse." Zach stepped back out of the room and let Jesse step in.

"Holy—"

"Monkey butts?" Zach asked with a smile.

Jess laughed. "I'm trying not to swear so much."

Zach crossed to the left side of the suite, and opened the door on another room that Jesse assumed was his room.

"You'll be right there?" Jesse asked.

Shiiiii--- Sheboygany hoober boobers.

She wasn't sure if her concern was how close he'd be in case of an emergency or how tempting it would be to have him so close. She had a feeling she'd be baking up a storm to try to get rid of all the pent-up sexual frustration the next six months were likely to cause.

I'll be the most practiced pastry chef in the world by the time we check out of this hotel.

"Do you need anything to eat, Jesse? I can call room service," Zach said from where he stood quietly across the room. He seemed to watch her intently, and she wondered if he were waiting for her to fall apart.

Jess shook her head. "No. I'm just gonna go to sleep, I think. If that's okay, I mean."

She knew she wasn't going to sleep. She just didn't think she could stand being in the same room with him for one more minute. The confines of the car had been enough. Jesse wanted some downtime. Time to herself to unwind and to try and get her body to stop the slow sizzle it had been doing since Zach Harris walked back into her world this afternoon.

"No problem, Jesse. I'll see you in the morning then," Zach said.

He checked the locks on the door and then slipped into his own room as Jesse turned to hers.

ZACH BLINKED BACK the sleep from his eyes when he heard a quiet knock on his door. He'd fallen asleep sitting up in bed watching a movie that wasn't particularly good when it came out in theaters. It wasn't any better on TV.

He looked up in time to see Jesse slip into his room. She was clad in nothing but a sheer pink nightie that only reached the tops of her thighs. It left little to the imagination. Zach couldn't seem to find his tongue as she walked toward him, all innocence and lace.

He watched, stunned, as Jesse reached for the hem of the nightie and pulled it up, uncovering a world of treasure – all for him. The gorgeous creamy skin of her thighs; the little valleys between her hip and her stomach that he knew would be sensitive to his touch, making her squirm and moan under him.

The soft, hot mound of curls covered only by a small pink scrap of fabric, so flimsy he could easily tear it off with his bare hands. Too shocked to question why she was here and what she was doing, Zach growled and lunged to reach for her. He reached out to pull her hot little body down onto his now very hard lap.

Zach sat up with a start when the sweet lacy concoction he'd dreamed up evaporated in his arms. He was left with nothing but the empty feeling where Jesse had just seemed to be. That and an erection he could pound nails with. Groaning, he lay back on the bed.

What the hell was I thinking? I can't get through six months of this.

But then Zach heard something else. It wasn't an intruder. He'd rigged an alarm on the door to the penthouse, and that hadn't gone off. Plus, he knew these sounds. These were the sounds of someone checking. Monitoring with a hypervigilance wrought from anxiety and fear.

The soft clicks as Jesse checked closets, locked and relocked doors, tore at Zach's heart. He stood and joined her in the living room. She turned when she heard him, and he watched the embarrassment wash over her face. He knew the source. She hadn't wanted him to know what she was doing. Zach put out his hand and took her smaller one in his.

"Come on, sweetheart." He almost winced as the endearment left his lips, but he kept a straight face for her. She wouldn't know he had never called another client sweetheart. That he'd never crossed such a line in his professional life before.

Get it together, Zach.

"Let's get you to bed." Zach led Jesse into her bedroom and pulled back the covers. He tucked the blankets in around her and then turned the light off in her bathroom. She lay in bed, watching him with wide eyes. He checked her closet. Checked under her bed, because he knew she needed that for now. Then he grabbed the comforter she had tossed on the floor. He stretched out as much as he could on the armchair in the corner of her room and pulled the cover up then turned out the lamp next to him.

"Good night, Jesse."

The room was silent for several minutes, and Zach began to think she'd fallen asleep. Then he heard a soft whisper come from her bed.

"Thank you, Zach."

Fuck me.

"Go to bed, baby girl."

Zach was tempted to bang his head against the back of the chair, but that sure as hell wouldn't look professional.

Fuck, fuck, fuck me.

CHAPTER 6

*T*he week before classes passed in a blur. Jesse was relieved to find she really liked Mary, the counselor Zach had found for her. Talking to her a few times that week had already helped. After four nights with Zach sleeping on the chair in her room, and then two with him on the couch outside her room, she'd felt comfortable enough to let him go to his own bed after he checked her room for her.

She felt better than she had in months, and was beginning to understand a bit more about her reaction to Kelly's kidnapping. Apparently, her reaction wasn't as uncommon as you'd think. People who witnessed loved ones go through a traumatic experience were often as affected by the event as the person going through it, just in different ways. She realized that her friend Jill's attack several months ago had only served to reinforce her fears, bringing her anxiety to new levels. She was a long way from wanting to go out without Zach by her side, but she felt as if she were making progress.

But today, Jesse's anxiety was spiking in a new way. Zach was about to teach her some self-defense moves. They'd help her get out of a situation if she ever did end up in trouble.

That meant being close to Zach. Having him touch her. Feeling the heat of his body as he came close to her. She'd been keeping as much space between them as she could during the week, but there was no way to avoid being too close for comfort this afternoon.

Jess felt raw, exposed. As if he'd be able to read the effect he had on her body all over her face. Would he figure out that she couldn't even breathe when he touched her? That her breath came in short pants and her palms got sweaty? That her heart raced and arousal balled deep in her belly? Of course he would. There's no way he could miss the signs.

Jesse jumped when Zach's knock came on her door. "You ready, Jesse?"

She took a few steadying breaths and opened the door. And felt her stomach flip. Those brown eyes of his looked right into her as if he could read her every thought. As if he knew her like no one else ever had.

Jesse knew in her head this was probably just a normal reaction for her to have to the man who was her only anchor to safety right now. Like patients who fall for the nurses who care for them. Or is it the other way around? Florence Nightingale falls for the patient? Oh hell, whatever. It was probably just a normal reaction people had to their rescuer. Because that's what he was doing now. Rescuing her.

Jesse nodded. "Ready."

"All right." Zach stepped to the middle of the living room where he'd pushed most of the furniture aside to create an open space for them to work. "We'll start easy today. We're just going through a few basic moves to get you started."

Oh, God, how I want to see his moves.

Jess bit her lip.

Shut up, brain. Just shut up. Self-defense moves. Nothing else.

"You okay, Jesse?"

Oh, God. He knows what I'm thinking. This is so embarrassing.

Jesse barely suppressed the squeak of humiliation trying to sneak through her lips and nodded, staring mutely at the hottie in front of her.

"If you're nervous, you just tell me, okay?"

Jesse nodded and Zach came around behind her, sending instant shivers of arousal coursing through her body. Jesse spun and stared wide-eyed at Zach.

"What're you doing?"

Zach laughed and lowered his arms. "Take it easy, Jesse. I'm just going to show you a basic technique for breaking away from someone who grabs you. It's an easy move for a beginner, so it'll give you confidence."

There was a little voice inside Jesse's head singing "Oh, my God, you're an idiot. An idiot. Oh, my God, you're an idiot, an idiot, an idiot."

"Oh…um…okay, then. Go ahead," Jesse said and she turned her back to Zach.

Zach put his hands on her shoulders and turned her back around. "You sure you're okay with this? It's all right if you're not ready for it."

Oh, I won't ever be ready for you to touch me. Well, wait that's not true. I'd love for you to touch me. Oh, hell. This is confusing.

Jesse smiled. "I'm good. I promise."

Turning her back on Zach once again, Jesse waited for his touch, willing the fluttery feeling in her chest and stomach to go away.

It didn't. It just spread to her legs.

Damn.

"Okay. I'm going to show you an easy way to break away from someone trying to grab you from behind. We'll practice what to do when you're grabbed from all different directions until you can get out of any hold. When I put my hands on your shoulders, I want you to raise both of your arms straight up in the air and then spin hard in a full circle letting your arms come down over mine. Go ahead and try it."

Zach put his hands on her shoulders. Jesse ignored the warm little zings running to all the happy parts of her body, and did as he instructed. She raised her arms, whipped around and down and broke his grip. Zach gently pushed at her back, sending her forward away from him.

"And, now you run from your attacker. You scream 911 as loud as you can, and you don't stop screaming or running until you get help."

They continued like that for an hour. They ran through the proper degree to kick at a knee for maximum damage, what points were most vulnerable to jabbing from knuckles or a key, and how to throw her attacker off balance.

The entire time, Zach's body was either pressed tightly against Jess's, brushing against it, or so close she could smell the incredible woodsy, spicy smell that drove her nuts when he was around. And he, unlike her, seemed totally unaffected. When he dismissed her from her lesson, she went to her room and tried to figure out just how the hell she could keep herself away from the only guy who made her feel safe.

Jess crawled into bed after a long hot bath. She pulled the covers up over her, wrapping herself in the soft silky feel of the high thread count sheets. She couldn't get the feel of Zach's arms surrounding her during their lessons out of her head. Biceps as hard as rocks pulling her close to an even harder body. As Jesse drifted into sleep, the memories became dreams, morphing into what she wanted instead of what had been.

Zach pressed his body along the full length of Jesse's, letting her feel the steel outline of his erection against the cleft of her bottom. His lips brushed against her neck, the feel of his breath on her bare skin sending shivers through her body and heat pooling between her legs.

Jesse moaned as Zach trailed a hand slowly, so slowly she thought she would die, zigzagging down her stomach, over her hip, then back to dive between her legs. His strong, solid hand cupped her, and Jesse writhed against it, willing him on, begging silently for more. Weeks of pent-up frustration poured through her as Zach kissed the back of her neck, then nipped gently at the back of her shoulder, mixing tiny droplets of pain with the pleasure, making her cry out for more.

ZACH STOPPED STILL in front of Jesse's door. He'd heard her crying out in her sleep, and came expecting to wake her from a nightmare. But, that wasn't a nightmare. The soft moans coming from behind the door had Zach hard and wanting in seconds. Not that he wasn't hard and wanting almost twenty-four seven living with Jesse. Zach let his forehead rest on the door as he mentally kicked himself.

He had no idea how he'd get through the rest of their time together. Keeping his hands off Jesse was getting harder and harder. The heated looks he doubted she knew she was sending him were becoming almost impossible to ignore. He'd had to be so careful when they were working together earlier, making sure his hips never came in contact with her. If she felt his reaction to her during those sessions, she'd know for sure what was going through his head. He didn't want her to know the truth. That he wanted her more than he'd ever wanted another woman.

A sensual cry came from the other side of the door, and Zach stepped back from the door as if burned. He needed space. Zach spun and crossed to his side of the suite, closing his door to try to shut out the sound of Jesse's cries. He couldn't answer them. He wouldn't take advantage of Jesse like that.

But the bedroom door wasn't enough to block her from his mind. He went to the bathroom and turned on the shower. Partly to muffle the sound, and partly to see if cold water would help. He knew it wouldn't. He'd been trying that for weeks now, and it hadn't helped a damn bit.

CHAPTER 7

Zach trailed Jesse everywhere. He waited outside her classroom when she was at school, and accompanied her anywhere she went outside of school. He also served as her guinea pig for new recipes for her bakery. Jesse wanted to offer a lot of traditional items, but she also wanted to offer creations that no one else had. That meant experimenting. A lot. Zach ate dozens of pies, cookies, cakes, tarts, croissants and éclairs.

Today though, Jesse needed tasters of a different sort. While Zach was working out in the gym, Jesse was playing around with a new idea she'd had for the bakery. Dog treats. She'd have one shelf in the cases devoted to bakery-style treats for dogs, made out of human-grade ingredients. They were designed to look like little pastries and cookies that humans would eat.

Jesse had researched the idea, and planned to mail some of the samples to Jack and Kelly to have their dog, Zoe, try out the treats. She also put together a packet of info for Jack to look over so she could get his take on the idea. Although organic and human-grade dog treats made up less than one percent of the overall figure Americans spent on their pets each year, the overall figure was fifty-five billion dollars. Jesse wanted to know if Zoe liked the treats and if Jack thought it was worth going after a piece of that one percent.

Jesse slid the last of her dog treat recipes off the baking tray and onto the cooling racks on the counter. She surveyed the samples and smiled. They were all either round, heart-shaped or diamond-shaped. She didn't make any of the typical shapes for dog treats like bones or fire hydrants. She'd designed them to look fairly similar to the Italian cookies she'd sell in the bakery. She'd dipped some of them in a carob coating, and had drizzled a peanut butter yogurt glaze over others.

Even though they were made with human-grade ingredients, they didn't taste anywhere near as good as her Italian cookies did. Jesse's Italian cookies were buttery and sugary. If she made the same recipe for dogs, she'd have a bunch of sick dogs and unhappy owners. So, she'd pared down the butter quite a bit, using yogurt instead, and they only had a bit of honey to flavor them instead of sugar. They weren't bad tasting. Just blander and dryer than her usual recipes. But according to her research, that would be just fine for dogs. She couldn't wait to see if Zoe liked them. She'd have to send enough for Kelly try them with Zoe, and for Jill and Jennie to try them with their dogs.

Smiling to herself, Jesse left the dog treats cooling while she went to take a shower.

ZACH CAME BACK from his workout famished. He was glad Jesse had become accustomed to the suite and felt safe there when he went to work out. It let him get away and clear his head of the fog she induced whenever he was with her. But, it was still nice to come back to some of her treats waiting on the counter.

Zach grinned and wondered how many he could steal without asking her. He shrugged. Even when she was making something for a class assignment instead of just her own experiments for the bakery, she usually made plenty extra for him. Zach eyed the little cookies and grabbed one of the chocolate-dipped ones and popped it in his mouth. He waited for the happy little taste explosion that Jesse's treats always brought.

And waited.

What the hell?

Jesse must have gotten the recipe wrong. These were pretty gross. Well, not gross. Just bland as hell. Her chocolate was always gooey and rich, with just the right amount of sweetness. If these were something she was working on for the bakery, Zach would have to find a gentle way to tell her she couldn't sell these things. Zach's stomach sank at the thought of disappointing Jesse. Before he could force the bland food down his throat, Jesse walked into the room.

When she spotted him eating one of the new cookies, her face broke out in one of those big, bright grins he loved to see.

Oh, shit. She's gonna ask me what I think.

"Trying the new cookies, huh? Like em?"

Zach saw the sparkle in her eyes, and knew these must be one of her recipes she was trying for the bakery. She was always so proud of them.

"Oh…um." Zach forced the bite of cookie down and looked at the tray of others sitting on the counter. "Are they something new you're trying?"

"Uh huh." Jesse was all smiles. "I'm sending them to Kelly to try."

That's weird. I usually try her desserts for her. Why would she send them to Kelly?

"Oh. Why are you sending them to Kelly? Are they special? Oh, wait, they're diet cookies, aren't they?" *That must be why they're so bland.*

Jesse put her hands on her hips. "I'm sending them to a woman, so they must be diet cookies? Is that what you're saying?"

"Oh…no…I mean…"

Abandon ship!

"And what on earth makes you think I would send diet cookies to a pregnant woman! Are you crazy?" Jesse sharpened her gaze, and Zach knew he was sunk.

Lifeboat? Flotation device? Anything? Anyone? Heeeellllllllp…

"Well, no. It's not that. It's just they're…um…" Zach looked at the cookie in his hand. "They're a little more… um…plain than your usual stuff. So I thought—"

Jesse's eyebrows shot up. "Oh, so now my cookies are plain. Keep going, Zach, you're doing a bang-up job here. Tell me, what did you think of the chocolate coating? Did you like that or was that bland, too?"

Stand still. Freeze. Maybe she won't notice you're still here.

Before Zach could figure out how to get out of the room without having to answer any more questions, Jess burst out laughing. She laughed at him as she grabbed the box sitting on the counter and started packing the cookies away. Zach watched, not sure what was so funny, but he knew the joke was at his expense.

"You should see your face. Trying to find a nice way to tell me they sucked."

Zach leaned a hip against the counter and watched Jesse. "Okay, what gives? Why the crappy cookies?"

That earned him a huge smile and a smug look from Jesse. "They're dog treats."

Zach dropped the rest of the cookie like a hot coal, incredulous. "You fed me dog treats!"

"Ha! I didn't *feed* you anything. You fed yourself. Next time wait for me to tell you what they are. Now," Jess smiled her sweetest smile for Zach. She picked up one of the treats with the peanut butter drizzle, "can you taste this one for me?"

CHAPTER 8

Zach watched Jesse come out of the school and search for him. He'd gone from waiting outside her classroom to waiting outside the school. Her therapist thought it was a good idea, but Zach worried the therapist and Jesse were both pushing too hard, too fast. He could always see a small flash of panic in Jesse's eyes right before she caught sight of him, and he didn't like it.

Jesse fell into step next to him, and they walked toward the coffee shop. They'd begun to stop there routinely at the end of the day.

"How was class?" Zach asked. Jesse always had funny stories of mishaps and suspected sabotage. Apparently, pastry school was a lot more cut-throat than Zach realized. The students hid ingredients on one another, swapped out similar looking ingredients to ruin each other's work, or rigged tools so they wouldn't work right. They all vied to be the teacher's pet. All except Jesse.

She seemed genuinely concerned when something went wrong for one of her fellow classmates. She stayed above the fray, just plugging away to finish the program. Of course, she had her own bakery to go home to, but Zach had a feeling Jesse wouldn't get involved even if she did need to compete for a job after graduation.

Jesse rolled her eyes. "Someone screwed with a bunch of the mixers today. They began smoking halfway through the cakes we were baking, and we had to mix everything by hand. My arms feel like they might fall off."

Zach's eyes dropped appreciatively to Jesse's toned biceps before he could stop them.

"Good practice for when the mixer goes out at your bakery someday?" he suggested hopefully, but in reality, he was beginning to wonder about all the 'pranks' at the school.

Jess laughed. "Yeah, sure. Way to look at the bright side. It's getting a little insane though. Switching ingredients is one thing, but this is going overboard. You should have seen the director. I thought her head would pop right off her neck when she came in and saw all the smoke. It was an expensive day for the school if they have to replace those."

Zach opened the door to the coffee shop and let Jesse in ahead of him. As usual, she went and sat at a table while Zach ordered, giving her just a tiny taste of being on her own. Zach ordered their usual: black coffee for him and a latte with three pumps of caramel for Jesse. They never ordered food. Jesse would whip them up something when they got back to the room. This stop was mostly just a chance for Jesse to get her feet wet being out in public without Zach right next to her.

Zach always kept one eye on her while he ordered, making sure she wasn't having an anxiety attack. He could see she was focused on her breathing. Her eyes flitted to him occasionally, but overall, she was doing well. He carried the coffees over to the table and sat next to her, reminding himself once again that he was here for business. Not pleasure.

"Do you think it's just one person doing all these things at the school, or is everyone in on it?" Zach asked.

She shrugged, eyebrows knitted in thought. "I don't know. I thought it was a few people at first. And, everyone seemed to be fair game. It wasn't as if any one person was targeted over others. I even had my baking soda switched for my baking powder one day. I've started tasting every ingredient before using them now. But, I'm beginning to wonder now if there's only one person. It just seems like things have gone past practical jokes. That seems like one person, you know?"

"Hmm." Zach nodded. He wondered how far this person would go and what the real payoff was. Why was it so important to make the others in the class look bad?

"There's one girl who's always a little too interested in what other people are trying in their recipes. She asks too many questions, and you can see her watching people over their shoulders. It's weird," Jesse said with a little shudder.

"I thought you all followed the same recipes?" Zach asked.

"Most of the time, we do. But sometimes we're supposed to tweak things. Find a way to make them our own. It's like Sharon doesn't have an original bone in her body, and she needs to see what everyone else is doing. Either that or she's really insecure and wants to watch everyone else. I don't know. Anyway, I thought it might be her, but her mixer was one of the ones that went nutty today, so maybe not."

"It's like you guys have this weird world in there that no one knows about. I never would have guessed it'd be so competitive," Zach said.

Jesse shook her head. "Me neither. I didn't have a clue until all this started, but apparently it's also competitive among the schools. The top schools vie for the best students, and all the best students are fighting for top spots in the best schools. That leads to the fight for jobs when we all get out. I think it might stop now though. Things went too far today. I bet whoever's doing this got a little freaked by the director's reaction."

"What are you baking for me today?" Zach asked with a grin, switching topics.

"Nothing." Jesse smiled.

"What? Why not?" Zach asked, his face falling. He'd come to rely on the handmade goodies Jesse made every day.

"No baking. Cooking today."

"I don't get it. What's the difference?"

"Baking is desserts and things. Well, that's not true. Technically, it means you cook something by putting it in an oven. For our purposes, what I mean is that today I won't be making desserts. I want to work on some of the lunch items tonight. The bakery will have a small selection of sandwiches and soups. It'll be a pretty limited menu, so I need to make sure things are unique and really good. I thought we'd try some paninis tonight. A Brie and Black Forest ham with spicy mustard and caramelized onions. And smoked turkey with Gouda cheese and a walnut olive spread."

Zach's mouth was watering, and his stomach started demanding attention as Jesse spoke. He pulled her up by the hand and headed for the door, with Jesse laughing behind him.

"It's not funny, lady. You can't talk like that and then expect me to wait while you relax and drink your coffee. That's pure evil, woman."

Zach didn't slow down until he got Jesse back to the penthouse where she followed through with a "dinner" made of the bakery's future lunch samplings. Perfection as usual.

CHAPTER 9

Zach laid his head back on the couch and rested his eyes. He needed to stay awake until he heard Jesse go to bed. He had a feeling tonight wouldn't be easy for her. And he didn't believe Jesse when she told him she wasn't upset by what happened that evening.

Zach's mind flashed back to the scene as they made their way home from Jesse's therapy session that evening. It was a perfectly normal incident for New York City streets. Four drunken men stumbled out of an alley and ran smack into Jesse. There wasn't any threat. Zach had stepped right in to intercede when the men circled her, laughing and stumbling around.

It was Jesse's reaction to the incident that worried him. She'd panicked. Although he knew that was totally normal, *she* didn't know that. Zach also knew she was probably beating herself up about it. Either way, he wanted to be sure he was here if she needed him tonight.

Zach heard the shower shut off in Jesse's room. For once, there was no flash of the image of her stepping naked and wet from the shower. Or wrapped in nothing but a towel.

There was no room in his feelings toward Jesse tonight for desire or anything sexual, just worry about her state of mind.

And that itself had Zach concerned. Because, what he was feeling toward Jesse was something he didn't want to examine. It was a powerful need to protect her, to comfort her, to prop her up and help her fight this until she was strong enough to fight it on her own. And, it bordered perilously close to a four-letter word beginning with 'L' that he didn't want to think about.

Minutes later, Zach heard the telltale whimpers coming from Jess's room, and he came wide awake. She could bury her head in her pillow all she wanted, but he could still hear her crying.

Zach knocked on the door. "Jesse?"

She didn't answer.

"Jesse? I'm coming in, Jess... So, if you're naked, pull those covers up."

Zach cracked the door and saw Jesse huddled under her covers, hair still wet from the shower, tears streaming down her face.

Zach knelt down next to Jesse at the side of her bed.

"Hey, Jesse girl. You falling apart on me?"

Jesse looked at him with those big doe eyes that cut right to his heart. Of course, right now they were red-rimmed and swollen, but they still tugged at him.

"I froze, Zach. I thought I was doing so well, and then the tiniest thing happened and I froze," she whispered.

"It's okay, Jesse. First, it wasn't a tiny thing. They were big guys and you were surrounded for a second there. It's okay to be frightened by that. Second, you're gonna have good days and bad. Things'll go up and down for a bit until finally, you won't have the bad days. Just the good ones. That's just the way this works." Zach brushed her hair back from her face. She didn't look like she was buying his spiel tonight.

"Wait here." Zach stood and went to Jesse's bathroom and grabbed her hair brush. He returned to the bed and sat down, then pulled Jesse up to lean against him. He started at the ends of her hair, brushing out the tangles that had formed when she'd climbed into bed with her hair wet and uncombed. Zach felt Jesse relax into him as he brushed. He spoke in calm, soothing tones, willing her to relax into sleep. If he could get her to sleep, things would look brighter in the morning.

"Is this a service you provide for all your clients?" Jesse asked, a smattering of her typical smart-ass humor shining through.

Hell no.

"Not normally, no." Zach let his smile come through in his voice since she was faced away from him.

Jesse took a deep, shuddering breath. "I can't believe I froze up over something as minor as that."

"It's not about what you did in that moment, Jesse. That'll get better over time, I promise. What matters right now is what you do tomorrow. If you lay in bed and eat cookies all day, then you've lost. But, if you get up again tomorrow and go to school and don't let this stop you, then you've won. That's what you need to worry about now. Just worry about getting up again tomorrow."

Zach continued to brush her hair, smoothing it down over her shoulders, letting the motion soothe her. He stayed that way long after Jesse fell asleep. Just holding her. Breathing in her scent. Dropping secret kisses to her temple as she slept. And knowing all the while that he was in far deeper than he should be. He knew he should turn this assignment over to one of his other people and run like hell, but he also knew it was far too late for that. He was just plain screwed.

CHAPTER 10

*Z*ach and Jesse both danced around the sexual tension that couldn't be denied by either one of them. There was no way to pretend it didn't exist, so they both did their best to ignore it. Zach got Jesse signed up for a few self-defense lessons with a female trainer in the area. He didn't say why, but they both knew it was to avoid getting too close again.

Three weeks later, they'd relaxed back into an easy truce of sorts. Jesse let her schoolwork distract her. When her counselor suggested they could decrease their sessions to once a week, Jesse said she'd rather not. Not that she thought she needed two sessions a week. She just didn't want to have to fill another evening with Zach. The evenings when they were home alone together were the hardest to handle.

Sometimes they went to a club or coffee shop in the evenings, but of course, since she needed Zach to go with her to those places, it didn't really help get her away from Zach. It just made it a little easier to be around one another in public instead of the close confines of their penthouse suite.

A suite that suddenly seemed to be two hundred square feet, instead of the eight hundred generous square feet that it was.

The sad thing was, Jess liked being with Zach a lot. They got along. If you didn't count the crazy sexual tension, it was easy being with him. They liked the same things, laughed at the same jokes, listened to the same music. If they didn't have this weird babysitter/crazy-person-that-needs-help-living-in-the-real-world relationship going on, she would really want to date him. Sometimes Jesse wondered how long it would take her to no longer need him by her side. Then, how long after that it would be appropriate for them to date. Six months? A year? Never?

If he were her therapist, the answer would be never. But, he wasn't her therapist. He helped her in her 'treatment' or whatever this was, but he made sure she had an outside therapist to talk to. So, didn't that mean that someday it would be acceptable for them to date?

God, I hope so.

Tonight, she and Zach were home, but thankfully, he'd holed up in his room while she worked in the kitchen. She was working on an assignment for school and, so far, it wasn't going well. She'd burned her first batch of the supposedly easy pastries, and now needed more ingredients to try again. Most likely, if you paid attention to what you were doing instead of thinking about the sex-God hiding out in the room next to you, the pastries really *were* easy to make.

"Zach," Jess called out to Zach in the next room. "I need to run down to the store."

Zach came out of his room.

"What's up?" he asked, as if completely unaware of the fact that he sent her heart rate skittering into overdrive. He had on low-slung jeans and a T-shirt that stretched snugly across a chest meant to be touched as well as looked at.

Just not by your hands, Jess. Hands off the babysitter.

"I burned the filling for my mille-feuilles, and I don't have enough eggs to try again. Can we run out to the store?" Jesse asked.

"Your mooool foooles? What?" Zach deadpanned.

Jesse threw a dish towel at him, but she did crack a smile. It was hard not to with Zach.

"Shut up. This is serious. These things take over an hour of prep before they go into the oven, and it's already late."

"I'm sorry, Jess. I can't. I have a conference call with some of my employees in five minutes. We've been trying to get everyone on the call, and this was the only time we could get everyone together. It should only take about an hour or an hour and a half. We can go after. Or you could call the concierge and ask them to go?" Zach suggested.

Jesse hesitated. She hadn't been out alone yet, and she wasn't sure she wanted to try it, but she needed those eggs. And, as far as she was concerned, she wasn't calling the concierge. The hotel manager had told her she could call if she needed supplies, but she wasn't used to that kind of treatment and wasn't comfortable with it.

Jesse cast a glance out the window as she thought. Even though it was seven thirty, it was still light out and would be for another hour. The store was just two blocks. She could do that. She knew she could. Jess squared her shoulders and gave Zach a smile.

"No problem. I'll run out by myself. It's close by."

"Are you sure, Jesse? We can call the concierge if you're not ready," Zach said, watching her closely.

"Nope. I got this. I can do it." Before she lost her resolve, Jesse slipped her feet into her sneakers and grabbed some cash from her purse. Shoving her cell into her back pocket, she cast one more look over her shoulder at Zach, who nodded encouragingly before she walked out the door.

≈

Zᴀᴄʜ ᴡᴀɪᴛᴇᴅ for the ding of the elevator to indicate its doors had shut, and then grabbed his keys and took off down the stairs. He took the stairs two at a time, knowing he needed to beat Jesse down if he wanted to follow her without her spotting him.

It had been a calculated risk, telling her he couldn't go with her. He'd been afraid she'd call him out on having a conference call so late in the evening. He knew she wouldn't use the concierge to pick up her eggs, so he hoped she truly was ready to go out alone. But, he'd be there with her just in case she had an anxiety attack or needed him.

Zach stopped when he reached the lobby level, and cracked the door to the stairwell so he could see the elevator doors. Seconds later, the doors opened and Jesse stepped out. He saw her pause after stepping off the elevator. No one else would notice the two deep calming breaths she took before she began walking through the lobby, towards the large glass doors that would lead outside.

Zach smiled to himself as he followed at a distance. So far, so good. She didn't seem to be having any trouble. Zach always felt proud of his clients when they reached this stage, but with Jess, the feeling was a lot stronger than he wanted it to be. His feelings toward her had well overstepped the bounds of professionalism.

Last week, they'd gone to a nightclub to let Jesse practice being alone in that setting. When her friends had left her alone in a nightclub a couple of months earlier in Connecticut, she'd quickly spiraled into panic. Because of that, Zach had arranged both a "help me" signal with Jess and also an "I'm okay" signal, so he could be sure she wasn't frozen in fear.

It had taken all the strength he had not to jump in when

some douchebag in a shiny polyester shirt got more than a little aggressive in trying to pick Jesse up. But she'd been giving him her "I'm okay" signal and Zach respected her too much to jump in just to alleviate his own jealousy.

Jesse stopped in front of the convenience store and Zach ducked into a doorway. He saw her take those two calming breaths again and then open the door. He'd have to wait outside or she'd spot him.

Minutes ticked off and Zach began to get antsy.

Fuck. Maybe it was too soon. I shouldn't have pushed her.

Zach scrubbed his hand through his hair, and wondered if he'd sent her out when she wasn't ready. He hoped he hadn't just done more harm than good. Just when he was about to give away his position and head in to see if she needed help, he heard Jess's contagious laugh spill out over the sidewalk. He peeked out and saw her laughing and talking with a woman he recognized from one of Jess's classes. His heart melted in relief. He turned his back to her so she wouldn't spot him as she said goodbye to her friend and started back to the hotel.

Zach waited as Jesse passed by him. She was four people deep away from him on the New York City streets, so she didn't notice him as she walked past. He trailed her home and watched as she entered the elevator. Now came the hard part.

Zach took the stairs double time and was glad he'd been working out so much while he'd been living with Jesse. The workouts had served to burn off some of his frustration but right now, they also helped him beat Jesse to the top. He slipped his key in the suite door and made it to his room, just as he heard her come into the kitchen.

Zach smiled as he heard her humming while she baked. He'd have to bury himself in his room and pretend to be on a conference call for the next hour, but it was worth it to see her beat her fears.

Zach sat on the edge of his bed for another forty minutes, then figured that was good enough for his fake conference call. He stepped out into the suite to find Jesse finishing up the pastries she'd needed the eggs for.

"Hey, Jess. How'd the trip to the store go?" Zach leaned against the counter and kept his face neutral.

Jesse sent a knowing smirk his way and he knew he was sunk.

Shit. I let myself get distracted by her for one damn minute...

"You ought to know it went just fine, since you were following me." Jesse's smirk widened to a full grin and Zach couldn't help but laugh back.

"When did you see me?"

"Not until we were back at the hotel. I saw your reflection in the revolving door while you were waiting for me to go in ahead of you. So really, since I didn't know you were there 'til I got back, we can count it as my first successful outing by myself," Jesse said.

Zach let down his guard for a minute and pulled her into a hug. "I'm really proud of you, Jess. You're gonna do just fine now. We'll get you a few more outings on your own, and pretty soon, you'll be back to your old self."

And you won't need me anymore.

CHAPTER 11

*G*radually, Jesse began to take more short trips out on her own. Without Zach following. They planned it carefully. Zach might only take her part of the way to school and then let her make the rest of the trip herself. Or, he'd meet her at the coffee shop after class, instead of waiting right outside the door. She gradually reclaimed her independence, even going to her therapy appointments on her own a few times.

As Zach watched Jesse's creamy, tanned arms flexing as she stirred an enormous whisk over the stove, he knew their time together was coming to an end. Jesse lifted the whisk out of the saucepan and let strands of melting chocolate run back into the pan, then turned to add a pinch of something from a jar before lifting the whisk to stir again.

Chocolate sauce. God, what I could do to Jesse with a pot of chocolate sauce.

Zach could picture the sauce as he drizzled it over her soft, full curves. He'd let little droplets fall to her stomach, surround her nipples in the rich, sweet dessert before licking it off one drop at a time. She wouldn't need any between her legs. Zach suspected she would have her own sweet flavor. One he wouldn't want to cover with anything else.

Shit. This has to stop.

Zach cleared his throat. "So…um. How's school been? Any more crazy high jinks and shenanigans?"

That had the intended effect. Jesse threw her head back and laughed, just as he hoped she would. "What are you – sixty?"

Zach smiled, loving the sound of her laugh. He could begin to see what he imagined was the old Jesse coming back. She laughed more. She was sweet and caring, and she was beginning to look a lot lighter these days. She wasn't carrying the heaviness around that she'd had about her when he first picked her up in Connecticut.

"You know what I mean." Zach leaned back and put his feet up on the coffee table as he watched Jesse work.

"Yeah, I know. Well, the little stuff has stopped. The ingredients are all what you expect them to be, but there are still weird things happening. The other day, one of the freezers went out and everything in it melted. People were talking about whether it might have been done on purpose again, but I don't know. That would hurt everyone or hurt the school itself. There doesn't seem to be any point in that if it's just one of the students trying to get ahead of the other students. I think the heavy competition is leveling out. A few people have left the program. The people left seem to know where they stand in the rankings now, so I think trying to hold anyone else back to make yourself look good is kind of pointless at this stage."

Jesse pulled the pot of chocolate off the stove and grabbed a plastic bag of confectioner's sugar. She gripped the sides of the bag and pulled, but nothing happened. Zach watched as she frowned at the bag, then tried again, appearing to put all her strength into it.

"Need help?" Zach asked as he rose and walked over to the kitchen.

Jesse scowled at him making it hard for him to keep the edges of his mouth from twitching into a smile. She looked like a child stomping her foot and insisting that she can do it herself.

"I can do it," she said, further solidifying the image.

Zach just nodded and waited.

Jesse turned the bag a bit to try a different angle, pulling this way and that.

"I just thought I'd ask, you know. Cuz, I'm right here and all," Zach said, again gesturing for the bag.

"No, I've got it," Jesse said with emphasis. And, just then, she did get it – in a big way.

The bag opened and exploded with an enormous poof of the light, fluffy confectioner's sugar landing all over Jesse. In her hair, on her face, covering her from head to midriff in a light white coating of sweetness.

Jesse stood wide-eyed and startled. "Son of a biscuit!"

Zach tried to keep a straight face, but it was no use. Between the look on her face, the fact that she was coated in powdered sugar, or her bizarre attempts to avoid swearing, he couldn't keep the laughter from coming out. And once he started, he couldn't stop. Even when Jesse put her hands on her hips and started toward him.

"That's funny, huh? I'll show you funny, mister." She headed his way with her hands raised as if she'd just love to share the sugary mess that coated her.

Before he thought it through, Zach grabbed her wrists to stop her, but that brought him too close. Too close to the sweet goddess with the bewitching eyes that twinkled with fire when she was mad at him. Too close to the dangerously tempting scent of Jesse covered in sugar. Too close to her tantalizing neck, covered in the finest sheen of powdery sweetness that Zach knew would melt under his tongue.

His eyes narrowed in on the sweet curve of her neck, and his mouth watered in anticipation. Just one taste. One sweet lick to tide him over. To satisfy the burning desire he'd been fighting for so long. Instead of holding her back, Zach was using his firm grip on her wrists to pull her close. Close enough to taste.

The air thickened and heated around them, and Zach swallowed hard, knowing he was about to make a mistake, but utterly helpless to fight it. Zach dipped his head and slowly let his lips brush over the sweet, soft skin. When he licked his lips, he tasted the sugar and growled, going in for more. All thought was gone now. Zach feasted on Jesse, completely blinded to thought or reason, or what was right and what was wrong.

Because this – Jesse in his arms – felt so right. Zach pulled back and watched her eyes, waiting to see if she'd stop him. But she didn't. She stared at his mouth, and that only turned the heat running through his veins even higher, turning the air around them hotter by the second. Memories of Jesse's moans as she tossed in her dreams flitted through to him and he felt his body harden in response. And then there was simply no holding back.

Zach closed the distance, brushing his lips against Jesse's and feeling her soft exhale at the contact. He let his mouth cover hers and his tongue brush over her lips, seeking entrance. She gave it willingly and moaned as his arms came around her, pulling her into his embrace, pressing his body to hers. Zach slanted his head, deepening the kiss, and heard the soft, sweet moans he'd fantasized about in response. Try as he might, Zach couldn't stop himself now. There was no turning back as he felt Jesse press her body against him, pulling him further into her spell.

~

JESSE THOUGHT for a split second she was dreaming again. She was so used to her mind running off on fantasy trips when Zach was close to her that, for a moment, she thought for sure that was all this was. Then she blinked, and Zach's body was still pressed against her. He'd pulled back from the kiss to look into her eyes, but he didn't break his hold, didn't break the contact that let her know he was just as attracted to her as she was to him.

"We should get you in the shower," Zach said, his voice gruff and hoarse.

"Probably," Jesse whispered back, as just the thought of showering with Zach sent heat pooling between her legs. Then she snaked a hand behind his neck, letting it curl into the dirty-blond hair that gathered at the nape and pulled him closer. This time, it was she who began the kiss, but he took over, controlling it almost instantly, turning her knees to butter and setting her womb on fire.

God, how she wanted this man. And she had no intention of turning back on this now. Bad idea or not, it had already started, and she wouldn't stop it.

Zach broke with her lips and began exploring her neck with his mouth, his tongue. Little nips with his teeth that sent tingles racing through her body. He spoke with his mouth still against her skin, letting her feel the heat in his breath, the want in his hands and mouth.

"I've wanted this for so long, Jess. Every time I look at you, I dream of stripping off your clothes and carrying you to bed. Touching you. Tasting you. Burying myself in you."

Jesse trembled with each word. "Please," she whispered, and Zach answered by lifting her into his arms.

He carried her through the master bedroom to the bathroom and turned on the shower with one hand, never breaking contact with her body and his lips. Jesse felt nothing but heat racing through her, building in anticipation as Zach stripped her of her clothes. Powdered sugar still coated her everywhere, despite Zach's impressive efforts with his mouth.

Jesse stepped under the hot spray and watched as Zach pulled his T-shirt over his head. Jesse couldn't hold back a small moan. Her fingers itched to touch the solid muscles of his chest and stomach. She held her breath as Zach's hands moved to unbutton his jeans. She'd dreamed of this moment for so long and now it was only seconds away.

When Zach stood naked before her and slipped into the shower, Jesse thought she would burst from the need, the anticipation. She greedily ran her hands over his powerful shoulders and down to his chest as his hands explored her body in equal measure. When Zach reached her breasts and skimmed rough fingers over her nipples, Jesse's head fell back and she surrendered completely to him. When his mouth sought out one nipple as the other hand continued to tug and tease, Jesse lost all reason. There was no outside world, no anxiety, no right and wrong. There was only this moment, these sensations, this overwhelming need being met at last.

Zach reached over and shut off the water.

"I want to take my time with you in bed." He wrapped Jesse in a towel and moved them to her bedroom then laid her gently on the bed, as if he treasured her. Jess had never felt more special, more wanted in her life.

But Zach paused. He held his body above hers and looked down into her face. "Are you sure you want this, Jesse? Are you positive?"

Jess smiled and brought her arms around his neck, pulling his body down over hers even as she raised her hips to try to meet him again. "I'm positive. Absolutely, positive."

It was like letting loose a force above her. Zach made his way over her body with his hands and mouth. Jesse couldn't believe the heat and hunger burning through her.

How does he do this to me?

Being with Zach was so much more intense than Jesse had ever imagined. He ran the tip of his tongue over her nipple and then breathed warm air from his mouth, making her squirm and push her breasts toward him. He answered with a small nip of his teeth, tugging at her nipple until she cried out with the combined pleasure and pain of it.

Zach showered her with open-mouthed kisses until she thought she'd scream from the torture of it. Jesse wanted more. To feel the heat of his skin against hers. To feel him slip inside her, to fill her. Finally.

"God, Jess. You're so beautiful. So incredible," Zach whispered as he raised himself up to the top of the bed to meet her lips again.

Before Jesse knew what hit her, Zach had looped an arm around her waist and flipped them. He on his back with her straddling his hips. She pulled herself upright and smiled at the sharp intake of breath from Zach as he looked at her. But the smile was lost on her lips as his hands came up. Zach cupped her breasts, then raised himself up to capture a nipple in his mouth, swirling his tongue around until Jess felt as if he were swirling her brains around with it. She couldn't think. Couldn't function. Could only feel the sensations racing through her body.

Jess thought she would burst with wanting and need as heat swept through her. Zach kept one hand on her waist to steady her and brought one hand down between her legs. His thumb swept over her swollen core, the moisture greeting him as if to show him how ready she was for him.

"Zach," she gasped as his thumb rasped over and over. With one more firm suck of her nipple, Jesse was stunned at the sudden orgasm that hit her. The sweet release ripped through her body as Zach drew it out, until she collapsed on top of him. Her head was in a fog as he rolled her to the side.

"I'll be right back," Zach whispered, and the loss of him at her side was immediate and painful.

Within seconds, Zach returned. Condom in hand, he joined her on the bed once more. Jesse watched in awe as he sheathed himself. He was incredible. His taut body was tanned and lean, each muscle standing out as if sculpted by an artist's hand out of clay or marble.

Zach's body covered her, forearms cradling her head as he looked into her eyes.

"You're sure, Jess?"

Jesse just laughed. A raspy, needy laugh. She'd have to do serious damage to this man if he stopped now.

"Yes," she whispered. "I'm sure."

Jess reached down and guided him into her, then her breath hitched in her throat as he took over and eased in so slowly, she thought the torture would kill her. She felt every inch of him as he stretched her, pushing deep, making her arch into him to try to take him even further. It was absolute bliss.

Zach pulled back out just as slowly, then sank back to the hilt making Jesse writhe and moan. Nothing had ever felt as good as Zach did inside her. Nothing had ever felt so right. Jesse looped her arms around Zach's neck and pulled him down to catch his mouth, kissing him deeply as he began to plunge faster. She pressed her hips up to meet his strokes, feeling another orgasm building, coiling tight and ready.

ZACH COULD FEEL Jesse tightening around him and knew she was close, so close to coming again. She felt incredible. So much more amazing than even his fantasies had been. He focused all his energy on holding his own release back as long as he could, wanting to let Jesse come again. Zach lowered his head, grazing her nipple with his teeth as he sped up, plunging over and over into Jesse's sweet, mesmerizing depths.

Zach knew from the tingling in his spine, the tightening, he wouldn't be able to hold out much longer. She felt too good, too wet and hot and tight for him to hold on. Zach moved to her other nipple, sucking deeply, and felt her explode around him, taking him with her into oblivion. He pushed through, plunging again and again, drawing out her pleasure as long as he could, before sinking down on top of her, utterly spent.

They lay together, trying to catch their breath. After so many weeks of wanting, needing to know her taste, her touch, how it would feel to be inside of her, Zach didn't want to let go. He rolled to his side and slipped out of her, grabbing tissues from the nightstand to clean them both up. He smiled as she snuggled into his side and he tightened his arms around her, pushing away the guilty feeling that he'd betrayed Jack. That he'd let Jesse down by letting this happen. He didn't want to think about that now. About how this should never have happened.

But just as sleep snuck up to claim him, Zach heard Jess mumble two sleepy words that turned his blood cold. "My hero," drifted off her lips as she drifted into sleep and he knew in that moment, he'd made the worst decision of his life. She didn't want him. She'd just fallen for the idea of a savior, and he'd probably just set her recovery back by miles.

CHAPTER 12

*J*esse felt a smile play over her lips as she woke from the best sleep she'd had in months. She remembered the way Zach had looked at her when they'd made love. The way he touched her as if treasuring her, cherishing her. Jesse took a minute to let the memories of last night wash over her, then stretched and reached out to the other side of the bed.

Empty.

Jesse opened her eyes and saw Zach sitting in the chair in the corner. Before she could smile at him, her gut clenched, and she realized several things in the span of a split second. He was dressed and sitting in a chair instead of in bed with her. He looked like shit. And, he was looking at her as if he were about to break her heart.

Here it comes.

"Jesse—" Zach began, but she cut him off.

"What is this, Zach?" Jesse tried to keep her breathing steady, to keep the tears at bay. She knew what he was about to do, and she wouldn't let him see her cry.

"I'm so sorry, Jess. I shouldn't have..." He let his head hang and shook it as if he couldn't find words. "I should never have taken advantage of you like that. I shouldn't have let that happen, and I'm so sorry."

Now Jesse began to feel the stirrings of anger inside as he spoke to her as if she were a child or an idiot.

"If I recall correctly, and I'm pretty damn sure I do, there were two consenting adults in this bed last night, not just you. You're not responsible for my fucking decisions, Zach." When Jesse got mad, she tended to swear a lot, and she could feel a whole hell of a lot of mad coming on.

Zach still shook his head as if trying to turn back time and erase what happened. Or at least erase the knowledge of it in his head.

"No, Jess. You haven't been yourself lately. You're in counseling, and you've been working so hard to deal with your anxiety, and I'm supposed to be a part of that treatment plan. I crossed a line that I can't ever cross."

Jesse got up and pulled on a bathrobe. She fisted her hands on her hips and glared at Zach.

"So, what now? You're just going to pretend this didn't happen? We're just supposed to go back to the way things were and pretend neither one of us has any feelings for the other? Cause, you can lie to yourself and to me all you damn well please, but I know the truth. I know what I saw and felt last night – and it sure as hell wasn't nothing."

Zach stood, his calm demeanor only serving to fuel the anger Jesse felt.

"No, Jesse. I've called in one of my people to come finish the assignment. I've told Jack I won't be able to finish out the time with you. My replacement will be here soon."

Jesse felt as if her jaw must be on the floor. "You're leaving?" Now she really did have to fight to shove back the tears.

I will not fucking cry in front of him.

Suddenly, Jesse was so tired of feeling weak and needy. She was done needing people to help her get around. She'd made a couple of solo trips without Zach, and she could do it again. She was through with this.

"Fine," she spit out. "Have a great life, Zach."

Jesse didn't wait when he tried to talk to her again. She turned and shut herself in the bathroom. Only after she had turned on the water, shed her robe and stepped under the hot soothing stream did she allow herself to cry.

Five minutes. You can cry for five fucking minutes and then you're done.

ZACH WATCHED the bathroom door slam and felt like a part of him had just been torn away. His feelings for Jesse were nothing but genuine, but that didn't mean it'd been okay for him to act on them. He was always talking to his employees about this very possibility, telling them never to get involved with a client. He'd even fired one guy when he'd stepped over the line and gotten involved with someone he was supposed to be protecting.

How was Zach supposed to fire himself? He'd put himself on desk duty for starters. His people could handle any assignments that came in. Zach would take himself out of the field and handle the office for a while.

He walked into the living room just as the front desk called to let him know his replacement had arrived. After telling them to let her up, Zach went to the door of the suite and opened it, waiting for Savannah to arrive. She'd been with him since he opened his company six years ago and was a good match for Jesse.

"Hey Savvy," he greeted the tall blonde woman who stepped off the elevator. She had a duffel bag slung over her shoulder, just like the one he had packed by the door. They went inside the suite and sat down. He'd wait until Jesse came out, transfer her to Savannah and go.

They waited twenty minutes, listening to Jesse shower, slam drawers, run the hair dryer. Twenty uncomfortable minutes of knowing Savannah knew what he'd done. She wasn't stupid. He didn't need to tell her why he was taking himself off the case. She'd know he was a hypocrite who didn't follow his own rules.

The door to the bedroom opened and Jesse came into the living room, a whole lot of anger coming with her. Zach and Savannah stood. Was it wrong for Zach to be thinking how sexy and hot Jesse looked when she was pissed?

Yeah, that's probably not right.

Jesse looked at Zach, then Savannah, then back to Zach.

"Really? A woman? Were you afraid if you sent in a man, I'd fuck him too?"

"That's enough, Jesse," he barked out.

"No. It's not enough. And don't talk to me like I'm a fucking child." She ground the words out through clenched teeth.

Wow, she really sounds like a truck driver when she's pissed. That shouldn't be sexy. Should not *be sexy. Damn it.*

Jesse stormed to the door of the suite and wrenched it open. "The funny part is, you think I slept with you because I think you're a hero, but I don't. I think you're a fucking coward who isn't ready to face the fact that he has feelings for someone. Get out."

Jesse stood by the door a full minute until Zach finally decided there wasn't anything more he could say. This had been his screw-up. He'd have to live with the consequences. Right now, that meant having Jesse very pissed off at him.

Maybe even hating him. Not taking his eyes off Jesse, he reached down for his duffle bag, slinging it over his shoulder.

"Savannah, I'll call and check in later. Goodbye, Jesse."

And, with that, Zach walked away from the most incredible woman he'd ever met.

CHAPTER 13

*J*esse watched the door close behind Zach and took two deep breaths. Then two more. Slowly, she turned to look at the suite and the woman who stood watching her. Jesse couldn't believe someone had just witnessed that whole scene. A total stranger. She should be mortified, but she wasn't. Right now, she was pretty far past caring about that.

Jesse picked up the hotel phone.

"Hello? This is Jesse Bradley. I need to move to a new room, please."

Jesse was done with everything. Done staying in the room she'd shared with Zach. She was done hiding out in the penthouse suite with all its security and private elevators. She felt as if she were living in a gilded cage because she couldn't handle the real world, and she was done with that.

"Is there a problem with your room, Ms. Bradley?" she heard on the other end of the line.

"No, no problem. I'd just like to downsize to a single room, please."

"Will you be needing an adjoining room?" asked the voice.

"No. I don't need an adjoining room. My bodyguard will no longer be staying here."

"Very well, Ms. Bradley. I'll make the arrangements and send someone up for your bags."

"Can you give me an hour to pack, please?" Jesse asked, thankful it was a Sunday so she didn't have to be at school today. She'd have time to figure things out, get settled into a new room.

"Yes, ma'am. That will be fine."

Jesse hung up the phone and turned to Savannah.

"I'm afraid you can't get rid of me that easily, Ms. Bradley," Savannah said.

Ugh, she's talking in that tone of voice reserved for crazy people. I'm not fucking crazy!

"You're fired. Please leave," Jesse said.

"I don't work for you, ma'am. I work for Jack Sutton," came the calm answer.

Jesse stared at the woman for a minute and then picked up her cell phone. She hit one of the pre-programmed numbers and waited for her brother-in-law to answer.

"Hi, Jack! It's Jesse." She put on her bubbly, everything-is-great voice. She'd gotten good at that.

"Hey, Jess. It's great to hear from you! How're things there?" Jack asked.

"New York is great. School's been wonderful. Just a few more months and I'll be all set. How is the construction going on the bakery?"

"We've got the permits, and they broke through the outer wall. The windows look great. They built display cases right into some of the side windows, so they display straight out onto the street. It looks terrific." Jesse could hear the enthusiasm in his voice and felt a surge of love for her brother-in-law. She felt guilty having to rush the conversation along, but she needed to get this bodyguard out of her way and try to eat herself out of the funk that was quickly taking over her.

"That's great, Jack. I can't wait to see it. Oh, hey Jack. Can you please call Zach's company and tell them I don't need their services anymore? I'm ready to try being on my own now." She knew she'd get a fight from him but she was ready for it.

"Are you sure, Jesse? Is everything okay there? Zach told me he can't work the case anymore, but said he was sending one of his best people to take over. Is there a problem with the new person? It sounded as if Zach had to go handle something else, but if this new person's a problem, I can try to get Zach back or see if he can send someone else."

"No, no problem. I'm just ready to try being on my own two feet again." Jesse turned her back on Savannah. "I've been going out without Zach on occasion and things are fine. No panic attacks. Minor anxiety, but I can get through it. I'm just ready, that's all." Jesse held her breath, knowing she needed to convince Jack if she were going to get rid of Savannah.

Jack's response came slowly, after a long pause.

"Okay. If that's what you want. I'll call Zach and let him know. But listen, you call me if you feel like you want them back. It's no problem. I want you to be comfortable. Promise?"

Jesse smiled and turned back to Savannah. "I promise, Jack. I'll call if I need them again. Thank you!"

Jesse hung up the phone and went to the door once again. She hoped for the last time.

"That's it. You've been relieved of duty. You are officially fired. Now get out."

Savannah picked up her bag and left without a word. Jesse took a deep breath. Alone. Finally. She leaned against the door and closed her eyes. She wanted to cry, but she'd had her five minutes. She'd pack her bags, move to her new room and then figure things out from there.

～

JACK FROWNED at the phone for a minute and then hit his wife's name in the contacts.

"Hi, Jack," came her sweet, sultry voice over the phone. The voice he'd never tire of hearing.

"Hey, sweetie. You feel up to a trip to New York? I thought we might grab Andrew and Jill and go visit Jesse for the weekend." In reality, Jack wanted the girls to visit Jesse to make her feel better, and he wanted to pay a visit to Zach. Something wasn't right. First, a message from Zach saying he couldn't work the case, then an all-too-chipper call from Jesse saying she didn't need a bodyguard anymore. Something was up, and Jack wasn't going to let his sister-in-law deal with things on her own again. They'd all screwed up before when they failed to notice something was wrong with Jesse. He'd be damned if it was going to happen again.

CHAPTER 14

*J*esse had settled into her new room, called room service to order more food than she could possibly eat, gorged, showered again and was now watching Sixteen Candles on some crappy cable channel. And, beginning to feel like crying again. She really liked Zach. A lot.

Even though they hadn't technically dated, they'd spent a lot of time together, and she didn't want to think about what it would be like to be without him. She missed him. And she'd really hoped... Well, it doesn't matter what she'd hoped. It wasn't gonna happen. Nothing was going to happen with Zach again.

And that sucked.

She was well past the cursing, angry stage and into wallowing in self-pity. If she didn't have school in the morning, she'd see if Kelly could come pick her up for the weekend. Suddenly, Jesse wanted her sister. She wanted a shoulder to cry on and someone to tell her it would be all right, even though she knew it wouldn't.

A knock on the door startled Jesse, but the voice she heard through the door was even more surprising. *Kelly.*

"Jesse, it's me. Me and Jill. Open up," Kelly said.

Jesse ran to the door and threw it open.

"What are you doing here? You're not supposed to travel, are you?" Jesse asked Kelly. At this stage of her pregnancy, Kelly wasn't supposed to travel more than an hour away from home, so New York was a bit of a stretch.

Kelly brushed her off. "I'm not that far out of the no-fly zone, as Jack puts it. Besides, there was no way in hell I wasn't coming when Jack told me something was wrong."

Jesse couldn't believe it. She thought she'd hidden everything from Jack on the phone. She took one more look at her sister and Jill standing in the doorway and lost it. She threw her arms around Kelly and let the tears flow. Kelly and Jill came in and flanked her on the couch, holding her hand as she told them how her day had begun.

"Oh, honey," Jill said, squeezing Jesse's hand when she had finished telling them how she'd kicked Zach out. "We've both been there. I know it hurts right now, but if it's meant to be, things will work out. And, if it isn't meant to be, you'll heal. I promise you will. It just takes time."

Jesse knew in her head Jill was right, but her heart felt as if it'd been run over by a Mack truck. She just wanted Zach to change his mind. To take back the words that showed he had no faith in her, no confidence in her to know what she felt, what she wanted. She wanted to rewind it all and somehow come out with a different ending. Because this ending just hurt too much.

ZACH SAT at the bar in the hotel lobby nursing a beer. Shoulders hunched, he stared down at the reflective surface of the polished mahogany bar. He wanted to kick himself for the way he'd handled things. If only he had been able to control himself until the job was over. He could've waited a couple months until Jesse was back into her routine and then connected with her again. He wouldn't have had to worry that she was just projecting feelings of hero worship instead of having true feelings for him. He wouldn't have to feel as if he'd betrayed Jesse. Like he'd betrayed Jack Sutton's trust, a man who'd placed his trust in him with both his wife and his sister-in-law's care. And he wouldn't have to feel as if he'd lost the best woman ever to come his way.

Damn it. He wanted a shot with Jesse. A chance to see if there was something real there. To see where things could go with them. Because he had a feeling things could be great between them. And he'd lost that shot because he was too weak to keep his dick in his pants.

Savannah had called and told him Jack Sutton had supposedly let her go, but he hadn't received a call from Jack yet so he'd wait for the official word. It was no less than he deserved though. A voice behind him pulled him out of his thoughts and had him shooting up off his bar stool.

"I don't know, Jack. He looks like someone stole his favorite puppy. Maybe you should go easy on him," Andrew Weston said as he leaned against the bar next to Zach.

Jack Sutton stood just inside the door, hands low on his hips, glaring daggers at Zach. The bar was empty, but the bartender watched them warily.

"Hey, Jack," Zach said, running a weary hand through hair that looked as if it would fall out if he didn't leave it alone soon.

Andrew stepped in front of Jack. "You look like shit, Zach. Wanna tell us what happened? I promise I'll keep him on a leash for you."

Zach heard a growl come from Jack, but he knew he deserved it.

"No," Zach said.

"No?" Jack bellowed behind Andrew, but Andrew stood his ground and Jack didn't move to get around him.

"No," Zach repeated. "I don't want to tell you what happened. I can't tell you what happened. I won't do that to Jesse."

Now Jack moved and got right in his face. Zach didn't move. Didn't flinch.

"Seriously, Zach? You slept with her, didn't you? I asked you to help her and you slept with her!"

"Uh, Jack," came Andrew's voice behind them, but Zach ignored it and apparently so did Jack because he stayed right in Zach's face.

Zach didn't say anything. He just waited for Jack to hit him. What the hell could he say? He'd fucked up so bad, there was no fixing it. That's why the sound of Jack's laughter shocked him so much. He looked up to see Jack laughing and Andrew grinning like a fool behind Jack.

"What?" Zach asked. "How is this funny?"

"Does she know you love her?" Andrew asked.

"Or were you too stupid to tell her?" Jack chimed in.

Zach just looked at them.

I'm an idiot.

"I'll take that to mean, 'no, you didn't tell her and yes, you're an idiot.'" Jack walked over to one of the empty stools and sat down. He raised two fingers to the bartender and nodded at Zach's beer indicating he wanted two beers for he and Andrew.

"Okay, spill it. If you didn't tell her you love her, what did you tell her?" Jack asked.

"That I made a mistake. That I shouldn't have taken advantage of her misplaced feelings of hero worship." Zach winced as he said it, realizing how arrogant and idiotic the whole thing sounded.

Jack and Andrew were grinning like fools, confirming Zach's worst fears.

"I really screwed up, huh?"

"Oh, yeah. This is like...new-diamond-necklace level of screw-up, not just flowers and a sad face," Andrew said.

"Oh, no. This is groveling on the floor level," added Jack.

Jack took out his phone and sent a text message.

"What are you doing?" Zach asked.

"Asking Kelly if it's fixable," came Jack's answer just before the chime indicating a new text message. Jack winced.

"We've gone from crying to ticked-off and back twice already," Jack read to Zach.

Three more texts came in quick succession, indicated by the tiny chimes going off one after the other without pause.

Jack read the stilted language of text messages. "Pretty bad. Maybe fix but needs to be something big. Think—" Jack stopped, not finishing the last text.

"Think what? What did she say?" Zach asked.

"Think she's in love," read Jack.

Zach grinned. "All right. Then I just have to figure out how to grovel, how to get her to listen to what an ass I am. How do I do that?" He looked back and forth at the other men expectantly.

Unfortunately, two very blank stares looked back at him.

"Um, we rescued our wives from crazed kidnappers. I don't think you can use our approach," Andrew said.

Zach sighed and fell back in his chair, head in his hands. He stayed that way for several minutes, until he knew what he had to do.

"I got it," Zach said, standing and heading toward the door.

"You wanna run it by us?" Andrew asked.

"No time. I need to get to Jesse." Zach kept going. He didn't plan on stopping until he was with Jesse. Not even for his two biggest clients who could probably make or break his business. One of whom, with any luck, just might be his family someday. Nope. Not stopping for anyone.

CHAPTER 15

*J*esse had finally stopped the flow of tears. She, Kelly and Jill were now eating ice cream sundaes from room service and watching *The Breakfast Club*. It was apparently a John Hughes marathon day. Just as Ally Sheedy began filling in her landscape with dandruff—a scene that made Jesse both laugh and cringe at the same time —there came a knock on the door.

Jill and Kelly looked at each other.

"Probably Jack and Andrew," Jill said. "I'll get it, Kelly. You stay put."

Kelly was eight months pregnant, so she got dibs on keeping her seat, and Jesse was given special treatment as the one nursing a broken heart.

Jill opened the door with Jesse following behind her.

There stood Zach, flanked by Andrew and Jack.

"Jesse," Zach started. He looked around Jill to where Jesse stood, with those sad brown eyes that could melt her heart in an instant. Jesse knew she should fight it, but she felt a flip of hope in her stomach and her heart started tap dancing in her chest. Or maybe that was the ice cream and junk food she'd consumed in the last few hours.

"God, Jesse. I'm such an ass."

"Wait, this is your idea of big? We said it needed to be big, Zach," said Andrew from somewhere out in the hall.

"This isn't big at all, Zach," said Jack, also speaking from the hallway. "When we said big, we meant a surprise of some sort. Jewelry. Flowers, at least. A poem. Something. I don't think he gets it, Andrew."

"Jeez, Zach. You should have told us you needed help. We would have rented you a helicopter. A limo at the least. Something. You need to whisk her away on a surprise vacation. Anything. Fuck, you went with nothing," Andrew continued as Zach just stood, eyes on Jesse, looking more miserable than she'd ever seen him.

Kelly stood—with no small amount of effort—and waved her hands at the boys. "You two. That's enough. Jess, we'll take Tweedle Dee and Tweedle Dum here home so you guys can talk. And no arguing over who's Tweedle Dum. It'll only make you both look bad," she added to Jack and Andrew as she moved past Zach to the other men.

Jill and Kelly wrangled Jack and Andrew down the hall, and Jesse took a step back to let Zach in the room.

She thought she'd feel angry, but her mad had long ago left the building. It was replaced by a big old case of relief mingled with longing and hope.

She watched as Zach seemed to collect himself.

"I screwed up and I'm so sorry," he said. "For the last month and a half, I've been telling myself the signs I saw from you were only because I was helping protect you. I kept telling myself it wasn't real. And, at the same time, my feelings for you were getting stronger and stronger." He took her hands in his. She let him but didn't say anything to him.

She just waited, watching.

He took a deep breath, before going on. "I was so incredibly happy when you told me you felt the same way, but then I freaked. I just kept thinking you'd wake up a month from now or two months from now and realize you didn't really love me. That you just fell for me because of the circumstances, and I knew I couldn't take that. I wouldn't be able to handle losing you. So I told myself you couldn't possibly feel for me what I feel for you after such a short time."

Jesse cleared her throat. "And what exactly do you feel for me?"

Zach brushed the back of his hand down her cheek, tugging her close to him with his other hand. "I love you, Jesse. I love you so much even though I know I shouldn't."

Before she could figure out what to say to that, Jesse heard a voice shout through the door. "Tell him you love him too, Jesse!"

Jack.

Good grief.

Zach banged on the door with his fist. "Shut it, Jack. I got this."

The sounds of Kelly and Jill trying to usher Andrew and Jack away came through the door, but Jesse didn't take her eyes off Zach.

Turning to her, Zach lifted her hands to his mouth and kissed each one. "Yeah, Jesse. Tell me you love me too. Please, God, tell me you love me, too."

He looked so hopeful, she didn't have the heart to make him wait any longer.

"I do love you," she said calmly, then narrowed her eyes at him. "And, someday I'll forgive you for being an idiot. But I think I'll make you pay for a while first."

He grinned, then grasped her hips and pulled her in tight to his body, a teasing glint lighting his eyes and his face.

"And what did you have in mind as payback, Jesse?"

She laughed and tossed her head back. "Let's start with a massage. Then maybe dinner in bed."

He dove for her neck, caressing it with open-mouthed kisses. "Then maybe…" Zach said as he blazed a path over her collarbone and down between her breasts, "…you'll let me love you all night long. Again and again and again."

His voice was a whisper, plea and promise all at once.

Jesse gasped as she wrapped her arms around his neck, pulling him tighter, willing him on. "Or we could skip the massage and dinner…"

He slipped his hands around to cup her bottom and lifted her as she wrapped her legs around his waist with a small yelp of surprise. And then his mouth was at her neck, doing those crazy things that drove her wild and sent heat to every part of her body.

Zach carried her to the bedroom and stripped them both so quickly, she felt like she blinked and they were standing naked in front of her bed. And, oh, how she loved being naked with this man.

He laid her down, pulling her hips to the edge of the bed as he sank to his knees in front of her. Almost instantly, Jesse was teetering on the edge of an orgasm, and he had yet to truly touch her.

Jesse moaned the second his lips came in contact with her. He kissed and nipped and teased, but didn't touch the one spot that would take her over the edge in a heartbeat. Jesse felt the sweet, achy build of an orgasm overtake her senses. Zach slowly slid one finger inside her, making her cry out and beg for more. She felt wanton and needy as she pushed down on his hand, trying to take what she so desperately needed.

She felt rather than heard a low rumble of laughter, and then Zach gave her more. Just as he slipped a second finger inside of her, he clamped down on her clit with his mouth, sucking as the sweet ache crescendoed into an orgasm that left her breathless and lightheaded.

And then Zach was there, sheathing himself and plunging into her, tripping off another orgasm as she clung to him, trying to keep some semblance of her wits about her, but with very little success.

When she finally floated down off the cloud he had thrown her onto, Jesse found him grinning like a damned Cheshire Cat as he still moved slowly inside of her. Still hard. Still building spirals of pleasure back up in her.

"Am I forgiven yet?" The whispered words sent more shock waves through her body as he plunged deeper and deeper. Jesse could do nothing more than gasp and dig her nails into his shoulders for several seconds before answering.

"You're certainly making some headway."

And then Zach sent her up and spiraling off into oblivion a record-setting third time, coming with her this time, before they collapsed on the bed in a tangled snuggle of arms and legs.

*****

Jack, Kelly, Andrew, and Jill walked into the suite they had booked in the hotel.

Before separating to go into the separate bedrooms the suite held, Kelly looked at Jack and Andrew. "You guys really wanted him to borrow a helicopter for some grand gesture?"

Jack shrugged with a grin. "It would have been romantic." He tugged Kelly toward him, closing her in his arms. "Romantic gestures are good."

"Speaking of romantic gestures," Andrew said, even as he and Jill started walking toward their bedroom, "when are we going to do something to push Chad and Jennie toward each other?"

Chad was Jack's cousin and the head of security at Sutton Capital. Jennie worked for him, but anyone who saw them knew there was something simmering between them. For whatever reason, the couple hadn't done anything about it yet.

Kelly shook her head. "That might not be a good idea, Andrew. There are things you don't know about in play there."

Jill put her hand on Andrew's chest and pushed him toward the bedroom. "You can debate this another night."

The couples each turned to their rooms, but Andrew called out over his shoulder. "I don't think we should let them keep ignoring what's happening between them."

Jack laughed. "We've created a monster."

Kelly sighed and pulled him into the room. They'd done enough matchmaking for the night. She smiled, knowing her sister was going to be happy. It meant the world to Kelly to see that.

CHAPTER 16

*J*ack officially fired Zach and his company, since Zach was no longer Jesse's bodyguard. Jesse and Zach moved back into the penthouse, so Jesse could have a kitchen again. Other than that, not much changed.

There was a lot more touching and kissing, and Zach did enjoy trying out Jesse's desserts in all new ways now. He was right about the chocolate sauce. And the caramel.

Jesse made Zach understand that he needed to talk to her next time, instead of making assumptions about what she was feeling or thinking. A week after finally taking their relationship from baker and bodyguard to dating and living together, Jesse was insanely content. Zach continued to walk her part of the way to school and to meet her after school got out. They spent a lot more time at the hotel together, and Jesse cut her therapy sessions back to once a week. She would likely switch to every other week soon.

There were still moments when she felt uneasy if she didn't have Zach by her side, but her therapist's relaxation techniques managed to ward off any full-blown anxiety attacks, and Jesse felt hopeful again. She knew she was coming back around to the person she'd been before.

As she waited for the light to change on her way to meet Zach after school, her mind played back the scene from the night before. They'd made love lying under a sheet out on the chaise lounge on their balcony, high above the bright lights of New York City. It was a little more subdued than some of their previous lovemaking, but it was no less hot. In fact, it was steamy and sexy, and just thinking about it again had her heated and flustered. It was then that she realized she didn't have her purse with her.

Oh hell. I mean, oh monkey butts.

Jesse had grabbed her bag with her dirty uniform from the long day in classes but had left her purse in the locker room. With her phone in it. Jesse cast a glance over her shoulder toward the school as she nibbled on her lower lip. She couldn't text or call Zach to let him know she'd be late. Should she run back on her own or go up to the coffee shop and grab him first?

After a second of indecision, she squared her shoulders. She could do this on her own. She turned and walked quickly, making brisk work of the two blocks back to school. She entered the quiet building and marveled at how silent it was after hours. There were still a few people in the offices, but once she reached the kitchens, all was eerily still.

As Jesse walked through the empty kitchen area, with the individual work stations all closed down for the day, she felt the hair on her arms and the back of her neck stand up. Suppressing a small shiver of unease, Jesse kept walking.

I will not let my fear overtake my life.

She began her breathing exercises and continued through the kitchen and into the adjoining locker room. Once inside the small area, Jesse went to her locker and spun the lock.

32 left.

16 right
7 left.

Jesse grabbed her purse and shut the locker, then grabbed her cell to check her messages and texts. Yup. Two texts from Zach.

everything okay?

getting worried...two more minutes and im heading ur way...

The last one was sent one minute ago. Jesse quickly sent a text back.

sorry! i'm okay. left purse and phone at school. omw now.

Jesse threw her phone in her purse and turned toward the door of the locker room. She froze mid-stride. There were voices coming from the kitchen. Angry voices. She peered through the door and recognized one of her classmates, Sharon. The man, she didn't recognize.

"No, Michael," Sharon hissed as she grabbed the man's arm. "This is too much. We can't do this."

Michael shook Sharon off his arm and continued toward the set of ovens closest to where Jesse stood. Jesse pressed against the wall of the locker room, listening but no longer watching through the crack in the door. There was no other way to get out of the room other than going past them. And a solid, bitter mass in the pit of Jesse's stomach was telling her not to let them see her here. Whatever was going on, it wasn't right.

"Michael," Sharon sounded desperate now. "This is arson. We can't do this. We'll go to jail if we get caught."

"No one will catch us. No one even knows we're here. We just need to rig one of the ovens and leave. If you'd taken care of things earlier like I told you to, we wouldn't be here, so just watch the door and quit bitching."

"No. I can't do this, Michael. I won't do this. It's too much." Sharon was crying now. Jesse could hear it in her voice.

Jesse's heart raced as she tried to hold still. She just needed to stay still until they left so she could get out of there.

She heard a guttural sound of frustration come from Michael. "Fine! Just go wait outside. I'll take care of this by myself."

Jesse heard footsteps as Sharon left the room and ran down the hall. She held herself rigid against the wall, steadying her breathing. And then she began to plan.

She thought through the scenarios Zach had taught her. The things she'd practiced in her self-defense classes. She took into account her position by the door and planned her defense if he stumbled on her location. He wasn't a particularly large man. Jesse prayed she could use that to her advantage.

Her heart felt like it would jump out of her throat any minute. She listened to the man she now identified as Michael swear as he tampered with the ovens only eight feet and one door away from her hiding place. And then the unthinkable happened. Jesse froze in terror as the familiar blast of Zach's ringtone piped out of her cell phone. The room went deathly quiet on the other side of the door, and Jesse knew she had only seconds to prepare herself.

She pressed the answer button on her phone and screamed.

"Locker rooms through the kitchens, Zach! Help!"

Then the door burst open and arms reached for her as she dropped her phone. Jesse didn't think after that. The motions came automatically as she whipped herself around, striking out at a forty-five degree angle just above her assailant's knee. Her instructor hadn't prepared her for the sickening crack and tearing sound that came from...what? Ligaments? Tendons? Jesse didn't know. As the man went down, Jesse brought her knee up to connect with his face, but it glanced off, and she lost her balance and toppled back onto the floor.

Michael screamed in rage, his face contorted in anger and pain above her as Jesse braced herself. She scrambled backward and brought herself up to a crouching position, waiting. Hoping she had it in her to get past him. As Michael charged, she held her position and prayed his knee was hurt as badly as she hoped it was. When he was almost upon her, she lowered herself, preparing as her self-defense instructor had shown her. When he threw himself at her, she came up under him, using his own momentum to throw him over her shoulder. Then Jesse ran.

She ran like hell and didn't look back. And, thankfully, as she cleared the locker room door and came through the kitchen, she ran straight into the safety of Zach.

He didn't break stride as he tucked her behind him.

"Police are on their way. Get outside and wait for me."

And with that, the door to the locker room opened. All hell broke loose as Jesse ran for the doors.

She didn't want to leave Zach, but she trusted him. If running is what he needed her to do, she'd do it. With what felt like lead feet, she ran through the kitchen and down the long hall to the door leading outside. The sunlight felt good after the stretch of moments trapped inside the locker room, but the fear Jesse felt during the attack didn't end when she got outside. Even though she felt proud that she'd fought off Michael, she was frightened knowing Zach was still in there with him.

That fear didn't last long. Minutes later, as police cars arrived at the school, Zach led Michael from the building. His hands were restrained behind his back and he was no longer fighting to get away.

Jesse watched in awe as Zach spoke to police officers, who placed Michael in the back of a patrol car. Then Zach's arms were around her holding her steady as she gave her statement to the police. The police would round up Sharon and bring her in for questioning. Jesse and Zach promised to come to the station the following morning to make official statements. From what they could gather so far, it appeared that Michael owned a rival culinary school that wasn't faring all that well. He planted Sharon in the class to try to disrupt things and chase students out the door. When she wasn't as aggressive as he would have liked, he planned to rig the ovens to blow up overnight.

As the officer walked away, Zach turned to Jesse and pulled her into his arms. "You did it, Jesse! You did it!"

She pulled back and looked at him. "Did what?"

He laughed and hugged her tight again. "You stayed calm. You defended yourself. You got out of there without a panic attack."

She let Zach's words and the feel of his arms around her sink in.

Yeah. I did do that.

And a small smile quickly grew into a big grin as Jesse absorbed the meaning of that. She'd fought back. She'd won. She was finally free.

READ CHAD and Jennie's story, Negotiation Tactics—the next book in the Sutton Capital Series here: http://loriryanromance.com/book/negotiation-tactics

ABOUT THE AUTHOR

Lori Ryan is a NY Times and USA Today bestselling author who writes romantic suspense, contemporary romance, and sports romance. She lives with an extremely understanding husband, three wonderful children, and two mostly-behaved dogs in Austin, Texas. It's a bit of a zoo, but she wouldn't change a thing.

Lori published her first novel in April of 2013 and hasn't looked back since then. She loves to connect with her readers.

For new release info and bonus content, join her newsletter at http://loriryanromance.com/lets-keep-touch/

Follow her on Facebook at
https://www.facebook.com/loriryanromance/
or Twitter at https://twitter.com/Loriryanauthor
or Instagram at
https://www.instagram.com/loriryanauthor/

Made in the USA
San Bernardino, CA
11 May 2018